PU

CHILDRE

In a primitive society of the future two children commit a crime which forces them to flee for their lives. Tia and Rabbit leave the cruel, oppressive community which is all they have ever known to find their way through strange unexplored territory to the sea. Their only guidance comes through their extraordinary telepathic communication with a man and a woman from a technologically advanced society, who are determined to reach the children before they are hunted down. Although brought up in a world of fear, Tia and Rabbit find that their mutual trust and friendship give them the strength to survive.

H. M. Hoover has created a starkly believable world slowly coming to life after nearly total ecological devastation. As explored by Tia and Rabbit it is both frightening and fascinating.

CHILDREN OF MORROW

H. M. HOOVER

Puffin Books

Puffin Books, Penguin Books Ltd, Harmondsworth, Middlesex, England
Viking Penguin Inc., 40 West 23rd Street, New York, New York 10010, U.S.A.
Penguin Books Australia Ltd, Ringwood, Victoria, Australia
Penguin Books Canada Ltd, 2801 John Street, Markham, Ontario, Canada L3R 1B4
Penguin Books (N.Z.) Ltd, 182–190 Wairau Road, Auckland 10, New Zealand

First published in the United States of America by Four Winds Press 1973
First published in Great Britain by Methuen Children's Books Ltd 1975
Published in Puffin Books in the United States of America 1985
Published in Puffin Books in Great Britain 1987

Library of Congress Cataloging in Publication Data
Hoover, H. M.   Children of Morrow.
Summary: After an unfortunate murder two telepathic children, members of
a primitive civilization, are led to escape by a friendly, unseen voice.
[1. Science fiction]   I. Title.
PZ7.H7705Ch   1985   [Fic]   84-23728   ISBN 0-14-031873-9

Printed and bound in Great Britain by
Cox & Wyman Ltd, Reading
Set in Baskerville

To Rosie,
with affection and gratitude

I

Tia could not see or hear him, but she knew he was hiding there in the bushes. His presence irked her. This was her treasure-hunting place; Sunday afternoon was the only time she had for herself. She had no wish to share either with Rabbit.

Months before, on one of her lonely walks in the wooded hills surrounding the Base, she had found this eroded mound. From its yellow clay gullies the rains had washed out beautiful pebbles. These she collected and hid, like a miser, in a hole at the base of a tree. Each Sunday she could steal away she came to look at her treasures and to search for more. But she could not do that now with Rabbit out there watching.

"O.K., Rabbit—come on out!"

Silence.

She sat down on a rock, elbows on knees, chin in hands.

"I'm just going to sit here and wait for you."

Her voice sounded very small in the hot stillness of the afternoon and for a moment she felt foolish. Maybe he wasn't there after all and she was talking to the trees.

A small wind rustled the leaves; a fly droned past. Somewhere in the hills to the east an insect began to sing and was answered by another. The sun beat down on her back and she could feel a trickle of sweat roll down her leg.

"B-b-boo!"

In spite of herself she jumped.

"Rabbit! How did you sneak up behind me?"

"I was j-j-just qu-quiet."

It was his unnatural quietness that had given him his nickname—that and his appearance. Like Tia, he wore a short sack-like dress of rabbit skins with slits for armholes and a drawstring at the neck. Rabbit was nearly nine but he looked much younger. He was a strange little boy, squat, barrel-chested, his head too large for his body, his eyes almost round. His appearance and speech made him the butt of the Family's jokes, most of them cruel. Their laughter had made his stammer worse with each passing year.

Tia, who was twelve, was slightly over five feet tall, as tall as any grown woman and taller than most of the men. Like Rabbit, her head looked too large, but only because she was so slender. With her narrow chest she found it hard to breathe when doing the heavy field work, and she frequently fainted. The Fathers did not feel her to be of much worth. Life was hard, and women must be strong to bear children and do the farming.

"Why did you follow me?"

"I f-follow you every S-s-sunday."

Tia digested this bit of information in silence. It did not please her.

"Are you mm-mad?"

She didn't answer.

"D-don't be mm-mad, Tia. I g-get lonely."

She glanced up and saw him looking at her with those great liquid brown eyes imploring her not to hurt him. In his face was the same loneliness she had already learned to disguise. "No, Rabbit, I'm not mad," she said truthfully. "Did you see where I hide my stones?"

He nodded, still looking directly at her, "B-b-but I won't t-tell! I l-looked at them, b-but I didn't touch—and I won't ever t-tell! Please b-believe me!"

"I believe you, Rabbit." She reached out and put

her hand on his arm. "Why didn't you just come with me when I went out on Sunday—instead of sneaking along behind?"

"Be-because I d-d-didn't think you wa-wanted me."

She smiled to herself, a strangely grown-up smile, and then, because she was a gentle child, said, "Next time—you come with me."

A big grin broke over the little boy's face and then faded abruptly as a thought occurred to him. "W-would it be O.K. if I m-met you at the t-trees behind the cowbarn? Th-they'll laugh if they see us g-g-going off to play together."

Tia saw how the pair of them would look in the eyes of the Base; Tia the Witch, tall and skinny, Rabbit so short and squat. The two freaks of the Family. She agreed. "Yes, Rabbit. That would be better."

Rabbit grinned again and relaxed.

"Tia?"

"Yes?"

"Don't you th-think we'd b-better go back? It's t-time for wa-worship."

She looked up at the sun; it was almost setting. They were probably late already and they were a long way from the Base. "We'd better run," she said, "they'll be mad."

They set off downhill at a lope, but Tia couldn't sustain that fast a pace. In no time her heart was laboring painfully and she had to stop to lean against a tree and rest. "You go on ahead, Rabbit. No sense you getting beaten, too."

"No. I'll ss-stay with you."

"That's silly, Rabbit. They pick on you too much now. There's no sense in making them mad."

"Don't you want mm-m-me?"

Looking down at the boy for a moment, Tia regretted being kind to him. Now he was going to follow her wherever she went and she would never be alone. But then she remembered how she felt sometimes. "Sure I want you—I just don't like you getting in trouble because of me."

"Tia?" They were out of the woods now and walking across the fields. "W-why do they call you a witch?"

"I don't know—the Fathers think I'm—" she paused for the right word and, finding it, rejected it. "They think I'm strange. I guess they don't like me, that's all."

"I g-g-guess they don't like m-me either."

"Oh, they like you, Rabbit. They think you're funny."

"I am n-n-not ff-funny!—am I?"

Tia grabbed his grubby little hand and squeezed

it. "No, Rabbit. I don't think you're funny at all."

"That's good," said Rabbit, "Be-because I don't think you're a wh-witch."

It was almost dusk when they reached the Base, a village built of logs. The houses sprawled in all directions around a central square. Here the larger trees had been left standing to shade the shaggy grass beneath. In the middle of this green stood the church. Made of rough stone piled over crumbling concrete, the church had no windows; its bell was housed in a log tower reached by a ladder. The church doors were ancient and so massive that they required the efforts of ten men to open them each Sunday.

East of the square stood the long community mess hall and kitchen; to the south was the L-shaped Fathers' House where the men who had sired children lived in the luxury of private rooms. On the other side of this building, away from the square, was the women's cabin, a large domitory. To the west stood the small schoolhouse, the common men's house and the boys' barracks. Both the Infant House and the girls' house were on the north side. Flanking these large buildings were the various work sheds, tanning sheds, cowbarns, granaries, corncribs, and outhouses necessary to the life of the community. There was no laundry, no store, and no inn. No stranger ever came to the Base.

As the children hurried up the dirt path toward the square, the last bell rang for worship.

"We're late."

"You go-g-go in ff-first, Tia. You can s-sit in the b-back with the women and th-they won't n-n-notice you're late, maybe. Mm-maybe they won't report you."

"How do you get up front without being seen?"

"Ssss-sneak!"

Tia tried to be casual when she passed the sentry at the church door, but he snarled, "You're late, witch," and she automatically assumed he would report her. She tiptoed into the low-ceilinged room and took a seat on the last bench beside the other girls. They ignored her.

The interior of the church was one large room. Along two sides of its massive cement walls, logs had been erected at intervals. They were not there as roof supports, but had been drilled to hold the torches necessary to light the interior. Split log benches served as seating; adult males on one side, women and children on the other. At the end of the room a log platform served as a dais. On it stood an ancient metal table and a wooden chair.

There was no stained glass, no picture, no decoration.

Tia felt someone brush by and from the corner of her eye saw Rabbit scurry past, crouched down behind the backs of the girls. When he reached the far wall of the church he dropped to his hands and knees and began to crawl forward to where the boys sat. She saw heads swivel as the women watched him pass and then quickly turned their attention again to the dais where the Major stood. But they were not fast enough. The Major glared at them in anger.

"I see the attention of the women is wandering. Of course that is to be expected with women. They have always lacked discipline." He paused for dramatic effect while the men laughed obediently at his sarcasm. During the laughter Tia saw Rabbit slip unobserved into the last row of boys.

No one in the community could have explained the source of the title "Major"; it had simply always belonged to the head man of the Base and to his Father before him. If a Major's sons could not sire sons, or if they proved sterile, they had no choice but to be soldiers or hunters, and a new Major was chosen by physical combat among the qualifying Fathers. This Major had won his title by force, back in the days when he was slender and adept at club fighting.

Tia was too young to remember a time before this Major, but the older people whispered that in the years of his rule things had changed at the Base. And not always for the best. It was true he was stronger and smarter than the last Major, they said, as it was true they lived in better houses and had more to eat—but he also made them work twice as hard. And sometimes when the adults were talking about him, they hushed each other when one of the children came around.

He was reputed to have fathered more children than any other man on the Base. That most of his children had died in infancy was a fact no one dared mention. The Major could be as cruel as he was greedy. He could order a man or woman whipped as easily as he could eat six rabbits, and with the same degree of emotion. And, they said, the older he became, the crueller he got.

Still glaring at the women who had offended him, he walked slowly the length of the platform, his long leather gown concealing the worst aspects of his bloated figure, but not his distinctive gait. The Major always walked as if powerful springs in his heels were threatening to throw him for-

ward on his face. His small eyes, red-rimmed from
the smoke of the torches, flicked over the rest of
the congregation. He smiled what Tia called to
herself his snakey smile, a grimace that pulled his
thin lips into tight bands of shiny flesh.

"Lack of discipline was the cause of the Destruction!" he suddenly shouted. "Like the women,
no one bothered to pay attention!" His face con-
torted into a feigned rage of righteousness, then
darkened as real fury took over. A trickle of drool
on his chin caught the light of the torches. Tia
felt a knife of fear run through her at the sight and
sound of him.

"Men had built a Paradise!" roared the Major
as he warmed to his favorite sermon. "But it was a
Paradise without discipline! Men built self-roll-
ing wagons so all might go where they wished.
And all went—everywhere—with no control.
With no discipline!"

"Men built houses taller than trees so they could
look out over the fields and be pleased. But always
came the cry 'Build them higher!'" He mimicked
a whining voice. "Do you see any of those tall
houses standing now? NO!"

"There is no discipline without work! Yet men
stored food and milk in containers so women would
have no work to do! You have seen the holy relics

of these containers in the sacred vaults. With no work to fill their days women painted themselves and wore clothing with such lack of control that men grew jealous and began to adorn themselves like women. And everyone wanted more! Always more! And was anyone satisfied? No!"

He was agitatedly pacing back and forth now as he shouted and each "no!" came out a little higher. Tia watched him with revolted fascination.

"None were satisfied! They always wanted more! The women grew bored and wanted to take over the duties of men. Men forgot what their own duties should be . . . and all for lack of discipline! And what happened?" He whirled to shake his fist at them in uncontrolled frenzy. "You all know what happened! You must live it every day!"

BANG! The fist hammered down on the table.

"Fools!" He poked an accusing finger at the congregation. "You complain that I am too strict! I know you complain—I've heard you whispering when you think I'm not around. And you anger Me as the old ones angered God!"

"When the old ones angered God he threw a plague over the earth and everything that walked! He turned the air to poison! He made the water foul! And for his lack of discipline, man was discharged from Paradise and left to die!

"Only the Ancient Fathers of the Base who worshipped the Great Missile were left alive! In His mercy he allowed our Ancient Fathers to take in and save women who would have surely died otherwise. Only by their discipline and obedience to their Major and to God were those people kept alive. And it is still only by discipline and obedience to me that you shall continue to live!

"When the anger of God lessened, when men could leave the Deep Shelter of this church, they saw the awful desolation, they choked on the thin air, their skins burned from the sun! They saw what lack of discipline had brought them down to—and they were frightened. And justly so!

"And God left the Missile beneath us as a warning and a reminder that if man should ever again try to rebuild the Paradise he once, in his weakness, built only FOR SELF-INDULGENCE, GOD WOULD EXPLODE THE MISSILE AND DESTROY ALL THE EARTH!"

As the Major ranted on, Tia's mind automatically shut him out. For as long as she could remember, at least every fourth Sunday had been spent listening to variations of this speech; how men had been tall and smooth-skinned, had breathed with no effort, how they had many animals to eat and fish were not poison, and all the rest. When it ended she knew they would have to go down the cold black tunnel and go down the stone stairway to the Deep Shelter and look at the Missile while the Major, still in his rage, would warn them of its awful power.

And that is what happened.

When the Major gave the command, the leather curtain covering the doorway to the Missile Chamber was pulled back. The men filed out by rank. First the Fathers, followed by the soldiers who supervised the daily work of the Base, then the hunters who, like the soldiers could never be Fathers, devoted their time to snaring game for the community. They were followed by the adolescent boys, then the women and children.

Two sentries carrying torches led the way along the tunnel and down the long stairs to where the ancient missile loomed, half-tilted on its side and corroding in the dampness of the underground vault.

Only the topmost portion of the missile was visible, the rest of its silo having long since caved in. It had become obsolete soon after its installation and its warhead had been removed. Any potential the missile ever possessed for destruction had moldered away generations before. Still the brutal strength of its shape and the myths they heard surrounding its origin made them feel a kind of awe.

The area around it was kept clear of falling concrete by the Fathers, and the walls of the chamber were kept in careful repair. The Missile was not polished because the Fathers were afraid to touch it. Their myths said it was forbidden to do so for fear of angering it and causing it to explode.

To Tia, the Missile was only another sacred relic, none of which she venerated. She had no more fear of it than she had of the rocks in the hills. But she was afraid of the Major and the Fathers. Because of that fear, she kept her beliefs to herself.

When all had come down the treacherous stairs and stood in a shivering group around the Missile, the Major took his place on the steps above them and his voice echoed even more powerfully in the vast dimness.

"Look on the Power of the Missile! Look on the Power of God! Remember His charity in saving your Ancient Fathers and be grateful!"

"Amen," chorused the people correctly. They stood then in silence in the semi-darkness, contemplating the shape above them while the Major exhorted them to obedience and discipline.

Tia was dreading the trip back up that long stairway. She knew she would be the last one up, as always, and would have to force herself not to faint from the effort of it. The air outside was thin enough—down here breathing was almost unbearable for her.

"Amen," the Major said again. That was the signal for their return to the surface. The Major was the first one up; the rest followed by rank.

As the women began to ascend the steps Tia looked up to see her mother halfway up the first flight and gave her a bashful smile. The young woman glanced down at her and then quickly looked away. Her first child was a source of extreme embarrassment to her. Rabbit's mother was the only other woman to have given birth to so strange a child.

Tia knew her mother was ashamed of her but she still blushed there in the dark at the bottom of the stairs. It was bad enough that she was so tall and ugly. That could be forgiven; many strange looking children were born. Fortunately most of them died in infancy. But when she was three or four, she couldn't remember now, the *knowing* had started, and after that, the Dreams. These would not be forgiven by the Fathers.

She learned to hide the *knowing* by merely keeping silent. The Dreams she told to no one after ridicule taught her to conceal her difference. But she remained suspect. She did things other people did not do, knew things it was not possible to know.

First it had been small things, like knowing when her mother wanted her, even though the woman had not called her, or carrying a rake out to the fields that her mother needed but had forgotten to take along in the morning. Tia had been four when she announced one day in church in a small but very audible voice, "The Missile is dead, Mummy. Why does that fat man keep saying it can hurt us?" She had been whipped for her blasphemy, and her mother received three lashes for not having taught the child respect. By everyone but the Major, the remark was credited only to a child's ignorance, nothing more. But the Major never forgave her for it and he personally saw to it that Tia's discipline was strict and her work almost unending.

It was the incident of the missing child which gained her the half-meant nickname of "Witch."

One afternoon in Rabbit's third summer he disappeared from the baby yard. Evening came and he still had not been found. Tia had been in the fields all day with her mother and the other women; they returned at dusk to find most of the men out searching for the boy.

Tia was setting the women's table when she

"saw" Rabbit. He was falling down a deep hole. His fear was so strong she nearly fainted with it. Dropping the wooden plates with a clatter, she had raced to the barn, grabbed a rope coil from its peg and, oblivious to the shouts of those who thought she'd gone berserk, ran across the fields and entered the woods. Her chest burned from running, briars tore at her, twice she stumbled and fell over creeping vines, but she got up and hurried on, Rabbit's fear dominating her mind.

Reaching the brush-obscured cave mouth she stopped and felt her fear diminish. Tying one end of the rope about a tree, the other about her waist, she pushed herself into the narrow opening and fell onto a stone surface. She picked herself up and saw Rabbit crawling toward her, apparently unhurt.

By the time the two emerged from the hole, her mother, along with some other women and a soldier, came running up to them. Baffled by their anger when they saw she had found Rabbit, Tia slipped and attempted to defend herself by saying she had "seen" him fall in. No one believed her. The Major himself questioned her for hours.

Neither she nor her mother were ever able to explain it. The Fathers suspected she had thrown him there herself; otherwise how had she known where to look? But when it was shown that was impossible, they were ill at ease. All the Major was able to get from her after repeated slaps was her insistence that she had seen the boy fall. The incident had become one of the Family's stories and Tia's possible guilt was still debated.

Only the fact that her mother had three normal children kept the woman from becoming an outcast. Tia knew her mother disliked and feared her for her oddness.

2

On Sunday night the younger boys were allowed to eat with the Fathers, it being believed they would benefit from contact with their superiors. But eating was all they were allowed to do; talking was forbidden, as was horseplay. Occasionally, if he was in a good mood, the Major would allow a boy to ask a question or two. But that didn't happen very often.

Tia saw Father Karl, the Major's first son and heir, glance up from his plate to see Rabbit grin at her as she entered the dining room with the bread tray. She gave Rabbit no response. Tia had learned from painful past experience that she was expected to serve, nothing more. Reaching the center of the wide table, she leaned across between fathers Karl and Neal to put her tray in its usual place. As she stepped back, Karl twisted slightly on his stool and snaked his right foot out. Before Tia could stop herself she tripped over it and fell sprawling to the floor.

"Clumsy thing, isn't she?" Father Karl said calmly as he speared a chunk of bread.

"You tripped me! You did it on purpose!" Tia's voice was angry and rather loud. "You put your foot . . ."

"Silence!" The Major's yell cut through her protest. "You should know by this time, girl, when you serve in the Fathers' House, you serve in the docility and silence fitting to the honour. Not with the tongue and temper of a witch!" Karl was his favourite son and could do no wrong. "You will apologize both for disturbing Father Karl and for your insolence before you leave."

Tia got up shakily and brushed off her arm. When her hand touched her elbow, she winced.

"I said, apologize." The Major's voice was dangerously quiet.

Tia looked around the long table. All the Fathers were watching her; the little boys were smiling in anticipation of seeing her get punished. All except Rabbit. His eyes were very big and round and his nose was oddly white. It was the look on Rabbit's face more than anything else that made Tia say, "I'm sorry for disturbing you, Father, Karl."

The sixteen-year-old man belched and went on eating.

"Get out now," said the Major, "and don't come back. You can be a dishwasher. I'm told Otto has more patience with rudeness than we do."

Tia left, seething with anger and humiliation, her face red with shame. Only the stupidest or most feeble were assigned to dishwashing. It was a pariah's job, on a par with shoveling the latrines.

In the kitchen she paused by the wash tubs to examine her throbbing elbow and discovered it was scraped raw and bleeding. Two small wood splinters from the floor were protruding from it.

"What happened?" Anna, an old kitchen servant, came over to her, took her briskly by the shoulder and turned her arm to the dim light from the overhead tallow lanterns. "You fall down?" The girl shook her head. "You were knocked down?" Tia didn't answer. "Well, however it happened, let's clean it up." The old woman carefully picked out the splinters, then got a soapy rag and none too gently scrubbed the abrasion.

"Ow!" The lye soap burned in the wound, and Tia's eyes filled with tears.

"Better hurt now than later," was all Anna said. "Now you go outside and sit on the bench and let it dry. Then you go to bed. I'll take care of your work."

"Thank you," Tia said in a voice hardly audible for she was afraid she was going to cry. She never allowed herself to cry. She was used to unpleasantness and could steel herself against it. But kindness was unexpected and disarmed her.

Escaping from the kitchen and the too-observant eyes of Anna, she ran across the grass. As she ran, little whimpering noises ached up from her throat. The sheltering darkness and the coolness of the night soothed her a little. Coming to the smokehouse, she sat down on the log bench in front and bit on her knuckles until the emotional storm was over. By the time she noticed her teeth were hurting her hand she felt better and got up and went over to the frog pond to wash her face. There was a series of plops and splashes as the disturbed frogs took to the water for safety. "It won't help you to hide," she whispered to them, "The Fathers will still eat you."

It was late and almost all the girls were asleep when she tiptoed into the Girls' House and slid quietly into her bed in the entry.

It had never bothered her to have to sleep in the

entry, even though it hurt her feelings to know why. The other girls, to win approval from the adults, found her full of faults. They complained she talked in her sleep, that she stared at them oddly, that she said strange things, that she was secretive, and they didn't know why, but they were afraid of her. The Major, not wishing to cater to the whims of female children, but saying he didn't want the girls' minds filled with blasphemous thoughts, had Tia's bed placed in the seclusion of the entry where she could not disturb the other occupants of the building.

Had it been done at her request, the location could not have pleased Tia more. At night when everyone was in bed and the door was bolted, the entry became a private room for her. Her bed, cold though it often was, became the source of her greatest pleasure, sleep. For in her sleep came the Dreams and the Dreams made her life bearable.

It seemed to her now that she had always Dreamed, and perhaps she had. When she was small and living in the Infant House with its often noisy nights, she had forgotten the Dreams upon waking. But as she grew older they became an almost nightly happening and she began to look forward to sleep.

They would not tell her the name of the place

she saw in her Dreams, only that it was far from her. They did not know how far, but it was somewhere beside a great expanse of water they called The Sea. There were windmills beside The Sea, not two small brown ones like the Base had, but a whole line of tall graceful mills with white sails. The houses in their valley were not made of logs but of something smooth and of many different colours. Except for the big house. It was white and built around a pool of very blue water and there were tall trees with strange big leaves only at the very tops. Ashira said they were palm trees.

For it was Ashira she "talked with" in her Dreams; Ashira and sometimes a man named Varas. At first Tia was afraid of Varas because she feared all men, but she had learned over the years to trust and love him. And once she dreamed that Varas told her he had feared her when he first received her dreams, that he had not thought it possible for anyone to have her power. When he said that, Tia had laughed out loud in her sleep and wakened herself with the noise.

She had learned to think of Varas as "The Teacher." She was not sure of Ashira's rank, only that unlike the women Tia knew, Ashira held a position of great power. Ashira said she was The Elite, the direct descendent of Morrow and chosen heir to the Gyrestone, the symbol sacred to the Balance of the One.

Tia did not understand what all that meant. But she had seen the Gyrestone often in her dreams, suspended from a gold chain about Ashira's neck. Around the deep blue centre of the gem's core, concentric rings of blue shaded from midnight to azure at its edge to rim in a blazon of long tapering blue-white crystals. When Tia looked at it, it seemed to her the rings moved like widening circles in a quiet pool.

Tonight, as he sometimes did, Rabbit slipped into her Dreams and started to tell Ashira and Varas about Father Karl and the Major. For the first time she noticed there was something odd about the way he spoke and when she asked him about it, he was surprised to see her. Then he said it was only a dream and he never stuttered when he dreamed. Ashira asked if they had ever before been aware of contacting each other. Tia told her that they talked to each other sometimes. But that was not what Ashira meant.

She told the children they must protect each other if they could, and that they must keep their dreams a secret, not even discuss them among themselves for fear of being ridiculed or punished. Her image was very solemn.

Rabbit thought vividly of all the times he, and sometimes Tia, had been punished. Upon receiving the scenes of those fragments of memory both Ashira and Varas recoiled, then, recovering their composure with effort, they sent out a feeling of great tenderness and sympathy to the children.

They had directed this feeling to Tia many times in the past. Now, as always, it made her wake up, ashamed to find she was crying in her sleep.

3

"Wait, Tia—don't go! Varas. . . ." Ashira turned to him, her eyes full of tears, her arms still outstretched to embrace and hold back. Her empathetic grief was like a cry piercing the old man's heart.

"Why does she do that, Varas?" Ashira began to pace the long, elegant room. "At the first hint of emotion—she deliberately breaks off! Why? To keep us from knowing her? Why should she need to create that barrier? The little boy could accept us."

"Yes, but you receive his images only rarely. And only through Tia. Tia's power is greater—as is, from what I can judge, her intelligence. She is never allowed to use either. Can you imagine any of us under similar circumstances?"

Ashira could and did—until Varas intervened and soothed her mind. His link with the children was through Ashira, enabling him to remain less affected by this extraordinary contact.

"From what Tia has shown us over the years," he reasoned, "we know something of the children's environment. It's apparently a society based on a few ill-remembered customs of a military post. Militaristic societies were primitive at best. And, unfortunately, in the old race of man, the individuals most likely to survive great catastrophe were seldom the most sensitive, or even the most intelligent. Merely the strongest in arms and stomach. The Macedonians prevailed over Persia, Rome over Greece, and the shaggy barbarians of the North over all. The people of the Base, unmutated, are the direct descendants of those barbarians. We know the culture and customs Tia transmits are vaguely traceable, but the degree of degeneration is hard to conceive. These are people with no art form, no music, no written history; people who worship the rotting remnants of a technological nightmare and live in fear of its power to destroy them. Just what Tia tells us of their religious beliefs is enough to make me long to study them. What possible theory. . . ."

"I am tired of theory, Varas!" Ashira's tone left no doubt as to just how tired she was. "I'm sorry, but we have listened to the Council's endless debate over theories explaining the existence of these people. And the debate always leads to nothing. You know yourself that Tia's thought patterns are not alien. Neither are the boy's—although his symbols are often infantile. But they 'think' like we do—they 'transmit' like we do."

"Granted," nodded Varas, "but all true telepaths transmit similarly."

"Perhaps, but we have no control to test that point. I suspect these two children are somehow linked with Morrow—but I have nothing to support my theory. . . ." She caught her friend's thought and smiled. They were back to theory again. "All right. I'll admit I've reached the point where I no longer care how or why they exist. They are there. They have extraordinary minds that will go to waste if they are not trained. And we can not train them from this distance. Tia can't even accept the fact that we are real. She still believes we are part of her fantasy life. How long will it be before she is forced to dismiss us and let her power atrophy? Or before her intelligence betrays her and she is killed for being something supernatural? I want to find those children!"

"We have searched the old maps," Varas reminded her. "Even if we could localize the girl's transmissions, we would still have no idea of the distance or geographical difficulties involved in reaching her. There were hundreds of missile bases in the old world."

Ashira picked up a soft woolen cape from the chair near the door, and he saw that she had dismissed his conservative logic.

"There is nothing before the Council this morning to demand my being there. I'm going down to the Master Library again. Somewhere in the memory banks. . . ." She paused, as an idea occurred to her, ". . . or maybe not?"

"Varas—it's too early to wake us all—I want every old book, record, tape, film—everything searched, especially any place where there might be old personal records judged too intimate or unimportant to put into the memory banks. Perhaps we have been looking in the wrong place."

As she went out, Varas sighed. Where did she get all her energy? Just linking with her mind on this distant convergence had exhausted him. Summoned from sleep by Ashira more than an hour before, he had come to her suite to be with her while she remained in contact with the children.

He was getting older, he decided; he disliked more and more having the even tenor of life interrupted by excitement. Nothing like this had happened during his term as Elite. Life had run smoothly as it had for years. Expeditions went out and returned with the same reassuring reports, "No trace of human survival." Morrow's settlements along the coast remained the only known human habitations. He had found this comforting. He had been glad when his term ended and Ashira came to power. It meant he could again devote time to his orchards and his music.

The sun's first rays made a spot of pink on the wall and he went to the balcony to look out. A flash of white caught his eye, and he saw Ashira emerge from the shadow of Morrow Hall and walk across the lawn to disappear among the trees.

He stood there, watching the sun slide above the blue clouds beyond the far hills and light the valley. The tiled roofs below suddenly glowed red. Beyond, the fields stretched green and lush, crisscrossed by irrigation ditches and canals fed by the river. Scattered among the fields the domes of greenhouses and poultry shelters sparkled in the sunshine. The bridges, high-arched to permit the passage of work barges, threw long shadows, as did the orchards on the slopes. From far down the valley came the morning sounds of the lifestock and the arrogant crowing of roosters.

Ashira reappeared from the pine groves and, catching his thoughts, she turned and waved to him.

She was following a path along a canal to the beach where the windmills hummed in the ocean breeze. Long ago the mills had been used to generate power, but after the completion of the new solar energy plant at the far end of the valley, they were kept only for their beauty and used to fill the desalinization tanks.

Beyond the windmills lay the pier where the ships of Morrow and her outlying settlements docked. One of the ferries lay at anchor. The ferry looked almost dwarfed beside the big *Simone II,* one of the pair of tri-hulled ships designed for research voyages. In the marina and scattered along the beach were various small craft built by individual owners.

Ashira crossed the brick road leading to the dock, climbed the wooded slope behind the lumber mill and went down a wide concrete ramp leading to a pair of heavy metal doors. At the smaller door she stopped and pressed a button.

A red light flashed on over the door; there was a faint hiss and the door slid open. Involuntarily the woman shivered, then walked into the airlock. The heavy door slid shut behind her. Another pause. A belltone chimed; the door leading from the airlock opened. She stepped through to the waiting elevator, touched light No. 37 and was swiftly carried down.

It was still too early for anyone else to be in the building. Inside, telephathic communication with the surface was impossible. Knowing she was alone in here always unnerved her slightly and she wondered, as she had many times before, how the people who lived out their entire lives beneath the surface had endured it.

Another belltone. The elevator stopped on Level 37. As the door slid open her glance automatically fell on the bronze profile on the huge plaque covering the opposite wall. How fortunate, she thought, that the profile was the only likeness of the founder of the House of Morrow. A short-necked man with drooping cheeks and eyelids, his only visible eye stared away into nothingness with almost manic intentness. It always amused her that the plaque had been mounted two years before the building's completion. She knew its inscription by heart:

Dedicated to the Memory of
SIMON ASHER MORROW

PRESIDENT & CHAIRMAN OF THE BOARD
MORROW INTERNATIONAL

Chief Executive Officer
MORROW CHEMICAL & PETROLEUM CORP.

President
MORROW DATA SYSTEMS INC.

Chief Administrative Officer
THE MORROW FOUNDATION

Former Assistant Secretary of Commerce for Science and Technology

In the decade preceding the period known as The Death of the Seas, Morrow, with the foresight, knowledge, and idealism typical of his approach to both business and life, along with his profound love for and belief in mankind, conceived and caused to be created this structure,

LIFESPAN,
the ultimate in protective human environments.

"I suspect 'human' was a term seldom applied to you, Simon," she told the image as she passed it. "And don't glare at me—remember, I've seen your corporate files. You were as great a monster as your esteemed namesake, Simone. But then both of you were necessary, weren't you?"

She smiled to herself at the power of egotism as she hurried down the hall. Pressure-sensitive cells in the floor acknowledged her presence by illuminating the hall before her and darkening it in her wake.

The Master Library was maintained as a room of the 21st Century with booklined walls, artificial windows richly draped, thick red carpeting, a comfortable sofa and two fat upholstered chairs. The room was dominated by a huge desk and massive chair that faced the door. There was a large viewing screen and, behind the desk, a computer that covered the entire wall. It had been Simon Morrow's personal auxiliary link to the central complex on the floors below. With it, if necessary, one could control the entire building.

Ashira swung the desk chair around to face the computer, curled up in the chair's leather vastness, pressed the audio-visual buttons, and settled down to work. All around her LIFESPAN went on functioning with its ancient efficiency.

Built sixty miles from the nearest city then existing, requiring more than fifteen years to complete, LIFESPAN was a masterpiece of electronic and technological genius, a subterranean complex, forty floors deep and a quarter of a mile square. Designed to be completely isolated from the surface in event of disaster, it was equipped with vastly intricate regenerative life-support systems. Its success in serving that function remained a tribute to Simon Morrow.

On either side of the complex, huge reservoirs had been sunk into bedrock. One held water, the other pulverized anthracite. When perpetuation of his own species was at stake, Morrow did not trust the fusion reactor that had brought his industrial empire such great wealth. Power was initially obtained from conventional generators; later, as danger of human damage to the surface plant disappeared, the metal plates covering the solar energy complex on the surface had been winged open to expose their intricately mirrored backs.

Descent from the then-hidden surface airlock was possible either by the endless ramp zig-zagging down the depth of the building, or by the elevators.

The upper levels were elaborate warehouses;

one level was a hydroponic farm fed on organic wastes, another was devoted to yeast growth and various fermentation tanks, a third floor held a select stock of domesticated animals and birds. There was a floor known as Morrow Park, a recreation area complete with real grass growing on real soil fed by artificial sunlight and sprinkler rain. There were laboratory and refinery complexes, a foundry, fabrication plants, a hospital, schools, theatre, central laundry, and even a "store."

On lower levels were the living quarters for the more than 200 scientists, engineers, physicians, instructors, technicians, and their families, all selected by Simon Morrow to share LIFESPAN with him. The basis for their selection had been simple; they had to be young, the best in their field, mentally stable, and parents.

The 37th level contained the Morrow apartment for Simon, his wife and their three daughters. Their quarters were adjacent to the Master Library and Master Computer rooms. On the lower three levels, protected like the vital internal organs they were, stood the computers, their great data storage banks, and the machinery basic to the life of the building's occupants.

These last four levels could, if necessary, be

completely sealed off and isolated from the rest of LIFESPAN. They had their own life-support systems and both separate elevators and stairs to the surface. Morrow had trusted no one, left nothing to chance. LIFESPAN had been built in an era of fear.

In the library now, the computer fell silent. Through no fault of its own it had taken Ashira up another dead end. It could not retrieve maps if it was not told which specific maps to retrieve. It could not compute available oxygen if it was not told the latitude, longitude, altitude and existing surface conditions.

In the past few years Ashira had gone over and over the data preserved on Simon Morrow's era, searching for a possible clue to explain the survival of Tia's people.

On copies of ancient film she had seen the seas turning gray, then brown and thick with scum; seen abrupt and bizarre climatic changes, watched the ugly clouds of smog layering in heavy stillness over the cities, endlessly drizzling dirty rain but failing to clean the atmosphere. As the oceans' enormous masses of plankton slowly died from the filth man continuously spewed into the water, as the oxygen supply generated by the plankton diminished and the air continued to be heavily polluted, as the plants and trees on the land sickened and turned brown or yellow before death, the chain began to break, link by link, and the slow suffocation of life on the earth began.

There was great panic as mankind finally realized the end was near. There was widespread rioting, starvation, disease. Suicide and murder took enormous tolls. But available records covering the decade known as The Death of the Seas indicated over 93 percent of all living creatures on the earth's surface and under the seas died by simple suffocation.

Admittedly the records of LIFESPAN held only scanty data about the actual living conditions on the surface during that period. The range of its surface equipment was limited. Before the decade ended the last of the orbiting satellites stopped transmitting. The men going up to the surface to observe were usually killed for their air tanks before they could regain shelter.

The few other people who survived had done so by escaping to entombments like Morrow's, readied in advance for disaster. But not so well prepared. Recent expeditions from Morrow had discovered the remains of one such subterranean dwelling. It had not survived the second generation.

Simon Morrow had planned well. During his lifetime his people functioned with the same efficiency as the building they inhabited. He established a benign dictatorship but gave enough responsibility and authority to a group of men and women called the Council of Ten to avoid the stigma of a dictator. He was a good administrator and a good leader. His people believed in him. Their joint goal was obvious: the eventual return to life on the surface. Until that could be accomplished, all they need do was work and have faith.

Simon Morrow died and LIFESPAN went on functioning. It took three generations for the order and discipline he established to falter and slowly die. Closed, confined by regimentation, the society began to stagnate and erode. Indiscriminate breeding increased the numbers of creatures dependent on the life-support systems. With overcrowding, loss of hope, and lassitude generated by poor diet and stagnant air, interest in learning and pride in accomplishment died.

Because of carelessness the torula yeast vats supplying the bulk of protein for all occupants of LIFESPAN became contaminated and the yeast's amino acids altered. At first the only result was diet deficiency. That was corrected by slaughtering part of the livestock on the farm level. But yeast was still consumed. Sometimes it had no apparent effect; other times it caused temporary madness or blindness. Some babies were born with massive kidney and renal malformations; other infants were extremely intelligent, almost frighteningly so.

The first recorded birth of a known telepath was a son born to the youngest granddaughter of Simon Morrow. There was no record of the father's name. Four years later a daughter was born who also proved to be telepathic. Geneticists termed both children mutants. The one remaining molecular biologist decided that the yeast was somehow responsible.

During the sixth generation, as far as Ashira could tell, lack of food and sufficient oxygen forced a partial re-emergence to the earth's surface. The air on the surface was pure again but so thin it could be endured for only limited periods. Those who managed to stay up long enough to do any exploration discovered few living creatures in the area except those near the edge of the sea.

In the tidal edge were clams, tiny gnarled oysters and huge scavenger snails. Inured to the poison of man's pollutants, adapting to limited oxygen, the shellfish had thrived on a world turned to garbage. In their systems through countless generations the chemicals had been condensed, refined and altered to forms never before known.

The people of Morrow, hungry for protein,

gathered the shellfish and snails, cleaned and cooked them, and found them delicious.

It was the snails that solved Morrow's population problem. They were as delicious as the extinct abalone was reputed to have been. The snails were eaten in great quantity, and were prepared in any number of ways. But within two years after they became a staple, the birth rate dropped radically. Infant death rates increased to over 45 per cent for females and 60 per cent for males. And it slowly became evident that many adults had become sterile.

The children who traced their descent from the three daughters of Simon Morrow seemed immune to some of the worse effects of the poisons. Those few who survived infancy grew up and had children of their own. The mutant gene proved dominant. In each generation, forced by the now necessary inbreeding, more children were born with great intelligence and the gift of telepathy. One of this children was Simone.

Had it not been for the emergence of Simone at this time, it is very possible that the history of Morrow would have ended on the doorstep of LIFESPAN. Of her own choice she had spent most of the first seventeen years of her life in the old Morrow apartment, studying the knowledge stored there, contemplating its adaptability to her own time. She had a brilliant mind and, more important, was the first telepath capable of concentrating transmission to a degree great enough to control, stun or kill. She never hesitated to use that power to accomplish what she felt was necessary.

Simone emerged at the age of 17 with the eyes, the energy and the ruthlessness of a fanatic. Systematically she began to build her new society. She based its laws on what she termed "The Balance of the One," the belief that all life forms on earth were individually and collectively only a portion of *one* great life form. To her, the examples of the past proved that destruction of one resulted in an imbalance and loss or eventual death of all. From the Morrow gem collection she chose the Gyrestone as her Symbol of State, feeling that it represented her idea in crystalized form. She named herself "The Elite" and decreed that the best mind in each generation would rule under that title.

The ten most intelligent and best balanced minds she appointed the Council of Ten and made them responsible for governing, for selecting new Council members and electing the Elites to follow. Any one with average intelligence and the ability to learn she sent back to the LIFESPAN schools to be "taught" by the computers. She made the study of genetics of prime importance during her lifetime and decreed that only the outstanding physical and mental specimens would be allowed to reproduce. She wanted telepaths and intended to get them. Simone herself had seven children by three different mates.

Before her death at the age of 81, Morrow Hall had been built, the remaining livestock and fowls were brought to the surface, housed and were reproducing nicely; fields had covered part of the valley and the people were beginning to build themselves homes in the village she had laid out. A secure and basically agrarian society had been established. For more than ten years before her death, Simone had trained her successor, a young man named Lyle Sandis, in the art of governing.

Ashira often wondered if, at Simone's burial services, the people of Morrow had felt not only grief and loss, but perhaps a little relief.

In the generations to follow, because of the order re-established by Simone and the ever-increasing number of intelligent telepaths among them, the people of Morrow gained a very real degree of "common sense." With their access to LIFE-SPAN's accumulated past knowledge and their ease in sharing information, they were able to both adapt from old technologies and develop new processes suitable to their time, and complimentary to the Balance of the One.

Ashira still could not understand why, knowing they were destroying their own world, the old societies could not have stopped it. Granted they were simple Talkers and therefore subject to irrationality and misunderstanding; still she believed they should have been able to halt their self-destruction. Or perhaps they were more stupid than she could imagine. If Tia's people were any example of the old mentality. . . .

4

When she finished drying the breakfast plates, Tia went out to the fields to join the rest of the women digging potatoes. As she passed the school she heard Father Neal shouting at the boys and was glad for the moment that girls did not have to go to school. The only person she disliked more than the Major was Father Neal. He had beaten her once when he discovered she knew how to read and write, and took from her the clay tablet she had made.

The women and girls were working at the end of the field by the woods, the stronger women spading up the potato plants with forks, the rest on their knees between the rows shaking the vines and pulling the tubers from the roots. The little girls put the potatoes into the willow baskets they dragged along the rows. Tia joined her mother and her three younger half-sisters in the row they were working. None of them greeted the girl when she dropped to her knees in the row behind them and set to work.

"You can start dragging the full baskets down to the end of the row," was all her mother said.

Tia looked up at her and nodded. She had expected as much. Everybody hated dragging. The basket handles were too short and you had to stoop very low to pull them across the cloddy ground. If you were not careful it was very easy to tug a heavy basket right across your bare foot and snag back a few toenails.

She stood up, looked over the field and decided to start at the far end. Actually, she thought as she walked down the row, she was just as glad to drag. Half the potatoes were full of dark red worms that scurried away on hairy legs, sometimes racing right over your hands in their panic.

She had dragged two baskets down to the sled at the edge of the field when she saw it—a glint of gold in a clod of mud. Picking up the clod, she crumbled it. In her dirty hand lay a gold ring, its circle filled with earth. Her first impulse was to run and show it to someone, anyone, in her excitement. But she quickly stopped herself. Someone would take it from her. She pushed out the earth that clogged its center and slipped the ring on the leather missile thong she wore around her neck. It clicked against the stone missle as she tucked it back under her dress. Then, feeling somehow guilty, she walked over to the next basket.

Two Simples and a soldier armed with a whip and club appeared by the sled. The Simples were men born with no minds; the Fathers used them as dray animals. It was their duty to perform the heaviest manual tasks about the settlement. Because they tended to be surly, they were always guarded by a strong soldier to see that they caused no harm. They slept in a locked room in the barn.

"Hurry up with that basket, girl," the soldier called to Tia. "We ain't got all day. These animals have to haul stones for the new cistern this afternoon."

Tia forgot about the ring and tugged the basket down the row as fast as she could. She heard one of the Simples give a snort of laughter to see her bending and straining as they did.

"Shut up!" roared the soldier. "You two—you get that other basket over there." He pointed and gestured for them to carry it back to the sled. They cringed at his shout and frowned at his command. "Over there!" He pointed again.

"Bring that here." Gibbering to themselves, they finally did as he commanded.

When eight baskets had been loaded on the sled, they pulled it away towards the potato shed, the wooden runners making shiny streaks over the grass, the Simples' muscles straining from the effort of pulling. Behind them walked their guard, yelling encouragement at them and flicking the whip over their shaggy heads.

When Tia had dragged all the baskets that were filled she went back to picking up potatoes. The bell rang for dinner and the women went in from the fields long enough to eat, then returned to their work.

After supper that night, when she had finished washing the wooden plates and cups from the Fathers' table. Tia sat down for the first time in hours and ate her own dinner with Anna and Meg, the other two kitchen helpers. Father Otto, the head cook, had gone to his room, his day's work done, and the women relaxed and talked among themselves.

Tia didn't even see Rabbit slip into the room. He was suddenly just there, standing beside the table.

"You give a person the creeps with your popping up like that!" said Meg, half starting up. Meg was an elderly woman of forty-five and her nerves were not what they used to be.

"Are you still hungry then?" Anna asked the boy.

He shook his head, yes.

Anna sighed and started to rise.

"I'll get him something," Tia said as she got up. "Want some roast rabbit?"

He nodded.

"You'd think you'd feel funny eating that," muttered Meg, "with your nickname and all. If it was me, I'd feel like a cannibal."

"Th-th-that's not my real n-name!" protested Rabbit. "P-people j-just call me that. I nn-never call m-myself that."

"Oh, and what do you call yourself?" asked Meg, enjoying the little boy's spunk.

"I w-won't tell you," said Rabbit. "It's mm-my own name and I w-won't tell you."

He took the plate Tia held out to him and sat down on the bench beside her at the table. After a moment of silence the older women decided that even though he was male, he was too young to object to anything they might say and returned to their conservation. Tia and Rabbit ate in silence until the adults finished their meal, washed their plates and went outside to sit and watch the stars come out.

"I wasn't really h-hungry," Rabbit said when the women had gone and they were alone in the big kitchen.

"No?"

"No. I had l-lots to eat. I j-j-just wanted to t-talk to you. I d-dreamed about you l-l-last night."

Tia was suddenly afraid.

"What did you dream?" she asked, trying to be casual, but finding it hard to swallow her food.

"This ff-funny dream with all ss-sorts of f-f-funny people in it. And you w-were it it—and you know what?" He didn't wait for her to answer, "I t-t-talked to you and I d-d-didn't st-st-stutter at all!"

Tia's heart went thump and then resumed its regular beat, but at a faster clip.

"What else did you dream?"

"That we were in a n-new p-place. And the houses were nn-nice, n-not like these. There was a w-woman who owned it all! She t-t-talked to me like she knew me." He paused a minute to wonder about that and thoughtfully rubbed his nose. "She had this stone around her neck—and there was a F-F-Father, but he was n-nice—You think I'm simple, huh?" he concluded suddenly, looking at the expression on her face as she got up to clear the table.

Tia said nothing. She didn't know what to say. If the Dreams were not Dreams—then what were they? If they were true . . . but how could they be true? Dreams were just something inside people's heads that nobody else could see. But how could Rabbit have her Dream?

"Maybe you had a nightmare about the Major and Karl?" she suggested finally, as she scoured the wooden plates with wet sand from the bottom of the wash tub.

"How d-d-did you know?"

"Want to see what I found today!" she said, wiping her wet hands on her dress. Desperate to change the subject, she withdrew the ring from its hiding place, slipped its thong over her head and held it out to him. "Isn't it pretty?"

"Yeah!" The ruse worked; Rabbit's voice was reverent as he stared at it. "L-look at that shine! I bet it's really old! Where'd you find it?"

"In the potato field. . . ."

The door behind them bumped open and both of them jumped as Otto tromped in. "What are you two little brats doing in my kitchen?" He caught sight of the ring. "Give me that!" he demanded and grabbed for it.

"It's mine! I found it." Tia said, glad the table was between herself and the man. At the first sound of Otto's voice, Rabbit had slid under the table. He emerged now on the opposite side and streaked for the door. There he paused, ready to flee. Seeing him scurry reminded Tia of his namesake and she grinned. It was the wrong time to grin.

"Don't you laugh at me, you ugly brat! Give me that ring!" Otto bellowed and held out a ham-like hand.

"It's mine," Tia repeated obstinately, although she knew she could not keep the ring now.

"I said, give it to me," Otto came towards her menacingly.

Tia backed away. "It's mine. I found it." But she didn't sound so sure of herself any more.

Otto reached out with one powerful arm and picked up a heavy skewer from the spit. "Put it on the table!" he yelled.

"What's going on in here?" demanded the Major, appearing in the open doorway. Behind him came Father Karl. The Major looked at the three of them and misunderstood the situation. "If you must fight with your kitchen trulls, Otto, learn to do it quietly. We are trying to talk."

"She stole one of the sacred gold relics," lied Otto. "I'm just trying to get it back."

"What?" The Major was obviously surprised that a girl would be that bold.

"She stole a gold relic!" Otto said again. He knew he would never get to keep anything so precious now that the Major knew it existed.

"I found it." Tia insisted doggedly. "It's not a relic. It's a ring I found in the field."

"Give it to me, witch," demanded the Major. He sounded excited.

"No!" She had not expected to say that, but having said it, immediately felt better. Faced with the three most powerful men in the community, she had stuck up for herself. There were few in the Family with that much foolish courage. "No," she repeated, "It's not fair. I found it and I should get to keep it."

"Get it, Karl," the Major said quietly, and stepped aside.

When the Major spoke, Karl, like the favorite son he was, instantly obeyed.

As she saw him come towards her, Tia stepped back, ready to run as soon as she had the chance. Karl circled the table on one side, Otto advanced around the other, his skewer ready to strike. The girl looked from one to the other.

"R-r-run t-t-Tia!" yelled Rabbit from the porch door. As he yelled, Otto threw the skewer and Tia

dodged. It hit the wall behind her and clattered
to the floor. As she raced for the door, Otto lunged
for her; he grabbed the hem of her leather dress
and then the thong with the ring, breaking it with
a twisting wrench.

"I've got it!" he announced triumphantly. Yanking Tia towards him, he raised his arm to strike
her in the face. She ducked the blow, grabbed his
hand and bit him as hard as she could.

"You l-l-let her go!" His scrawny arms flailing
in fury, Rabbit threw himself against the big man,
punching, kicking, hitting. Karl reached the struggling trio and grabbed for the girl, pulling her
away and yanking the ring from Otto's grasp.

"I'll kill her!" Otto shouted as he jerked Tia
away from Karl with one hand and knocked Rabbit to the floor with the other. "No little witch bites
me! I'll kill her!"

Otto struck her once and then as his arm flew
back to slap her again, he made a strange gurgling
sound. His arm fell limp and he crumpled to the
floor. Rabbit jumped on top of him, still hitting
away. Karl flung the children away from the fallen
cook.

Tia stumbled against a cupboard, dazed. For a
long moment she thought she was Dreaming, she
had such a clear impression of Ashira. Startled,

she reached up to touch her eyes. They were open; she was awake, her nose was bleeding, her lip swollen. She saw Rabbit picking himself up from where he'd fallen near the door.

"Otto?"

The Major and Karl were bending over the fallen man.

"Otto?" Karl dropped to his knees and put his hand on Otto's still chest.

Tia was aware that Rabbit had taken her hand. She was shaking with anger and fright but her legs still carried her as the little boy pulled her towards the outer door.

"Otto?"

She heard the Major's shout as Rabbit pulled her outside.

"For God's sake, Karl, didn't you see his eyes? They're full of blood! Medic! Medic!"

Rabbit gave her an anxious tug. "R-run!" he said, "I think I j-j-just k-k-k-killed Father Otto!"

They ran.

5

In late afternoon the intercom on the library desk chimed softly and Ashira reached over and flicked it on. It was Varas and he sounded excited.

"I'm sending a car down for you, Ashira. It should be at the airlock now."

"What is it?" Her mind sorted over the possibilities; a forgotten meeting? an emergency? a possible accident? That was the trouble with being isolated down here. . . .

"We've found a diary! I called a convergence after you left this morning and gave everyone your directive for an intensive search. As you know, the Sandis home has quite a collection of personal diaries—Lora Sandis set everyone to reading—"

"What does it say, Varas?"

"It confirms your theory—there is a link!"

"Why wasn't it in the memory banks?"

"Because the basis of the link was a perverse disregard for the Balance."

There was a short stunned silence on Ashira's part, then, "Do you have the book in your hands?"

"Yes."

"Read me the pertinent entries." She flicked on the desk recorder.

"It's from the personal log of Martin Sandis, Geneticist, Morrow Research Expedition #44 sailing 10/11/05 . . . let's see, Martin died, uhmmm . . . three years ago, I believe?"

"I know. Please, Varas, just read it."

"Very well. But first I must explain that, according to the diary, the botanists on the expedition established a base camp near the old San Francisco Bay area. They intended to remain there for some days collecting fruit trees. Sandis decided to take one of the amphibians on a small side trip of his own up into the nearby mountains. That is where I'll begin.

"Entry thirty-one—Hitaka should have come with me! Discovered a whole family of pigs. They looked weird enough to bring joy to her zoologist's heart. Great chests like barrels with ribs protruding. Nearly scared me to death when I flushed them from the underbrush. They disappeared before I could catch a specimen. Strange. Most animals unafraid of us. Must be instinctive memory. Have seen unusual number of rabbits. Appear healthy and normal. Am following an old roadbed up through the hills. Little remaining evidence of past human habitation.

"Entry thirty-two —Camped by river thru remains of city. Nothing left here but ruin. Depressing place. A few buildings still partially standing but too dangerous to enter alone, too far gone to justify going back to base camp and getting help.

"Entry thirty-three"—Varas' voice paused and Ashira could picture him scanning the page. "Nothing here worth bothering—he mentions passing a dam and what was once apparently a hydroelectric plant and then continuing on upriver. Then we come to the good part!

"Entry thirty-six—From a hilltop today I saw what I think were two men!!! At any rate they seemed human—they wore leather clothing. They appeared to be hunting and disappeared into the trees without spotting me. By the time I returned to the car and found a place where I could drive it up the riverbank, there was no trace of them. Am following the old roadbed again as far as the brush will permit me. Hate to leave the car. If they are human, they look primitive and possibly dangerous. I have not reported this to base camp. Are they going to be surprised when I come in with two of these specimens!

"Then there is a passage of two days with no entry.

"Entry thirty-eight—They were men! Discovered an entire village of them in a remote valley among the hills. Spent two days observing from hills by telescope. Apparently a communal society. Men hunt, women work in fields. A group of larger than average males appears to be an almost parasitic ruling caste. These people are small, average height 4'5", big chests, short legs. Hard to gauge intelligence. Attempted mental contact. No response.

"Entry thirty-nine—you can read this when you get here—it's merely a description of the village —the military base was apparently quite large— some observations of women working in the fields —notation of crops grown.

"Entry forty—Today I broke the law of the Balance of the One. But I did it in the interests of genetics. One of the younger female workers had wandered into the woods near my blind. Except for the fact that her skin felt like hide from over-exposure to the sun, she seemed healthy enough. I mind-stunned her and performed artificial insemination with File Morrow-strain sperm tubes. If it takes, if she reproduces, and if the child is a telepath, then its effect on this primitive society will be interesting to watch. Especially if our telepathic gene remains dominant with them. Upon due thought I have decided not to report this experiment as yet, but to wait and see the results when we return here on the next expedition in five or six years. In my opinion this settlement is not and can not be, for centuries at least, any threat to Morrow or to our Balance. As a study in human heredity it should prove most interesting. When the time comes and I learn the results of my experiment today, I will report this to The Elite in person."

"And that's it." Varas concluded. "The rest of the diary is interesting, what I've had time to scan, but these are the important pages."

"Why was a report never made—does he say?" asked Ashira.

"No. He kept the diary hidden—it was found with his other books and papers after his death and stored away unread. I would imagine that when he had time to think over what he had done, he realized the consequences to himself of making such an admission—not only his failure to report the finding of people, but the experiment he performed without Council approval."

"He said there would be a return expedition. . . ."

"One was scheduled to stop there and go farther north, but so little was believed found that our ships never went back."

"Does he have any direct descendants?"

"No." Varas knew her reason for this question. Ashira thought the man had been unbalanced. This had been Varas' initial reaction and he had immediately checked the records. "Upon twelve-year testing Martin proved to be sterile. He remained so. The records also indicate a distinct personality change after his return from the expedition. He gradually shut himself off from most minds and became more or less a recluse."

"With a great secret to hug to himself," Ashira said grimly. "I'll be right up—I want to read that book myself. Thank you, Varas."

At Morrow Hall he was waiting for her in her private study. A small cozy room, it contained the only fireplace in all of Morrow. The fireplace had been installed by Simone, the room's first occupant, in blatant disregard of her own laws. The tile floor was covered by a thick hand-tied rug of brown and orange, and the satiny smooth polish of the furniture reflected the rug's warm colors.

"I have called a formal dinner and a Council meeting for nine this evening," Varas announced as she entered.

"Thank you—I suppose you've also ordered a printout on Expedition #44?"

"Yes—along with all pertinent maps. Gene assures me they'll have it ready."

"Did Sandis leave any film of his discovery behind?"

"None we can find."

"What's the general reaction?"

"What you might expect—excitement, clinical interest. If we decide to send out an expedition I can tell you now that our biggest problem will be determining who must be excluded from the trip."

"Will you come with me?" Ashira asked, and Varas knew then that there was no question in her mind. It would simply be a matter of how soon they could prepare to leave.

"Of course. After all these years as her 'teacher,' it would be rude of me not to greet Tia personally, wouldn't it?"

Ashira gave him a look of loving amusement. "I agree—and I appreciate the personal sacrifice you'll be making. Suppose the peaches get ripe while we're gone and someone other than yourself picks the first of your Blushing Whites?"

"Don't worry, I intend to leave detailed instructions on their care," Varas said quite seriously. He had already thought of that risk. Those new grafts were his pride of the season.

"Now, where is the diary?"

"On your desk." He withdrew, leaving her in privacy.

Without changing from her daysuit, the young woman stretched out on the window seat and began to read, trying, as she did so, to fathom the mind of the author. He seemed entirely sane, happy, extremely interested in his chosen field of study. A whole person, well balanced. But why would he carry sperm tubes in his freezer pack on a research trip? How had he removed them from the inventory files of the Genetics Lab? And then another question occurred to her: Expedition #44 was made more than thirty-five years before. Tia and Rabbit were at lest second generation results of the breeding! Who were their parents—and what were they? Rabbit said his mother was dead—Tia's was still living. Did they both have the same father?

She nearly contacted Elaine, then, seeing the clock, restrained her impulse. There would be time to discuss this later. She looked down at the diary still in her hands and thought of the loneliness and isolation its recorded crime had caused for Tia and perhaps Rabbit, and the danger to which it would now subject Morrow. "You were wise, Martin Sandis, to escape me by death," she whispered to the book. And anyone seeing her face at that moment would have been left in no doubt as to who ruled Morrow.

Later she bathed and dressed for dinner. Her gown was of extreme simplicity, its silky white complimenting her deep-golden skin. Her only ornaments of jewelry were the Gyrestone and the supple gold wire she wound about her long black hair to bring it into a submissive coil over her shoulder.

As she stepped out of her door she met Varas coming along the hall.

"I was just coming to escort you to the dining room. I thought together we would make a truly impressive entrance!" He was wearing a deep blue one piece formal suit with a round gold collar and a belt of golden loops. Over his shoulders was a short cape of blue with a high flared collar that called attention to his beautiful blue-white hair. Before offering her his arm, he stepped back to survey her.

"Your appearance always pleases me so much, Madam. Truly lovely. I must say there are times when I regret our laws. That such a specimen as yourself should be restricted to three offspring seems a shame. And when the children are as beautiful as the mother—even the boy—and give every indication of being as bright. . . ." He sighed in mock sorrow.

"You allow your pleasure in esthetics to cloud your logic, sir." Ashira entered into the spirit of his banter with a formal little bow. "You must give due credit to the children's sire, to the remarkable skills of our geneticists, to the love of the children's nurses and, last but not least, to their esteemed teachers."

"You are too modest, Madam." Varas bowed in return and they started down the hall.

"I am also very hungry—and rather excited. Do you realize, Varas, after all this time, we are going to find Tia?"

Varas looked at her and his glance was shrewd.

"I suspect you feel she may prove to be your third daughter, Ashira—if not by bloodline, then by empathy. Much as you are mine."

"Would it be too unwise?"

"Loving is never unwise—so long as you see the object of your love as an individual and not as a distorted reflection of your own mind. We are a fantasy to Tia. Perhaps we have never admitted that she—and now Rabbit—are, in another way, somewhat of a fantasy to us?"

"You are right, as usual," Ashira admitted after thought. "Like yourself, I tend to suffer from idealism."

As he saw The Elite and Senior Counsel come down the stairs together, the Steward struck the huge gong in the hall to signal the serving of dinner.

Not until she saw the crowd in the foyer below did Ashira realize the full degree of excitement that the news of the diary had caused. Without exception every Council member was present, as were all the Staff Leaders. It usually took a Direct Order to pull some of these people away from their work in time for formal meals.

She saw Elaine, the Senior Geneticist, arguing with Foran, Senior Biochemist, about the merits of melanin. It was apparent that Elaine felt she was losing the argument; she had already begun to irritably finger the large yellow diamond she wore about her skinny neck. "I wonder," Ashira thought to herself as she watched the older woman, "is there something about being a geneticist that makes you power mad?" She dismissed the thought as uncharitable. But Genetics was going to be rather thoroughly checked when there was adequate time to do so.

On the steps outside, various younger staff members were noisily engaged in a discussion of the rising full moon and its effects on human and other animal psychologies with Mark and Jemmel, the two men who served as ship captains and marine biologists.

Homer, Senior Mycologist, was talking fungi with Jessica, his favorite pupil, and whomever else would listen. Occasionally he would be so taken with his own theories that he would retreat into convergent telepathy to convey their possible results—much to the disgust of those around him who found fungi less than fascinating.

The rest of the household members and guests were gathered in small groups or eyeing the food that Cleone and her staff were carrying to the dining room. Seeing Ashira and Varas approaching, the conversation broke off, all bowed to them and then filed into the dining room in their wake.

It was a delicious meal. Cleone's staff had gone to as much effort as if for a holiday occasion. There was Real Meat, small slices of beef lightly broiled over charcoal, braised mushrooms, snowpeas delicately seasoned and mixed with waterchestnuts, huge purple grapes, red pears and wintermelon and, for dessert, small cakes full of raisins. Since dinner was to be followed by a Council meeting, no wine was served. It had long ago been shown that alcohol produced an adverse effect on both logic and communication.

When she had finished eating, and as soon as it was polite to do so, Ashira excused herself and went to her office. She wished for some time alone to study the computer printouts on Expedition #44 before the meeting. Ten minutes later she summoned Varas with a symbol so urgent that everyone in Morrow Hall received it. There was a questioning murmur as he abruptly left the table and hurried from the room.

Promptly at nine the Steward entered the lounge and announced, "The Elite requests all Council Members and Staff Leaders to assemble in the Conference Room immediately."

Ashira was standing by her chair at the head of the table. Her face was pale with a fatigue that had not been apparent earlier. Varas sat slumped in the chair to her right, his chin resting on his folded hands, his eyes closed. Those who had been disturbed by her earlier call for him tensed a little at the sight of them both.

Ashira wasted no time on preliminaries.

"Mark, Jemmel—how long will it take to get the *Simone II* ready for our trip? We must plan for a total distance of approximately 6000 miles, allowing for slowdown and possible detours when we reach the portion of the sea to the north that still is fouled with slime molds. There isn't much chance we can avoid these—they appear to be on our most direct route."

"So that means 20–25 days. . . ." Jemmel figured.

"Depending on weather and how fouled the ship gets in that muck," added Mark. "How fast do you need her?"

"As quickly as possible. The children's lives are in jeopardy—by accident the boy lethally mind-stunned an adult male. The male was intent on beating Tia—to death, so the boy thought." By relaying visual images she showed them the portion of the incident she and Varas had received. The violence of the scene shocked the assembly.

"Savages, all of them!" Elaine's strong opinion blotted out the rest. "Shows you what uncontrolled breeding can do."

Her remark reminded Ashira, "Elaine, you are

aware of the contents of the geneticist's diary found today? Good—no, don't interrupt. I want a report from you later—say after this meeting?—on the probable results of Martin Sandis' experiment. I want to know if there could be other, less gifted telepaths in that community. If so, how many? Now, Mark, we were discussing the preparation of the ship. . . ."

"Are you taking amphibians? We'll have to allow for their weight."

"We'll take one. When the children are calmer and I can reach them, I will advise them to escape from the village and follow the river the diary describes to the coast. I don't know how far they will get. It's a rather desperate chance for them—but they are in a desperate situation. Their settlement is about one hundred miles inland. One car will carry enough of us to control anything human we might meet—if we have to go inland after them."

"Do both of us go?" Jemmel asked.

"Yes, we'll be traveling at maximum speed day and night. We'll need you both as captains. Do either of you object?"

Both men agreed they wouldn't miss the chance to go.

"Good. Mark, you will be responsible now for general equipment. Jemmel, you will see to individual and specific supplies. Lora, you will go as ship's doctor. I want the hospital and lab fully equipped and staffed—or as fully equipped as the captains will allow you to make it without over-burdening the boat."

"We'll need an isolation chamber. They may have unique bacteria," decided Lora.

"Granted, but Expedition #44 discovered nothing like that in soil samples or animal tissue cultures. But there is always a possibility. Check the records and then decide. Now, as to the rest of the staff, it will consist of the ship's regular crew—you are experienced and cover most of the sciences. Varas will go as my aide. In our absence the remaining Council members will have full authority with Foran as Senior Counsel-in-Charge. Can the ship be loaded in three days' time?"

6

They had passed the barns and were halfway across the cornfield before they realized that no one was after them. Tia's lungs forced her to slow down, they were burning painfully. As she jogged along gasping for air, Rabbit suddenly stopped. He stood very still, listening. Grateful for the rest, Tia caught up to him and stopped, too.

"What do you hear?"

He shook his head as a signal for her to be quiet, then turned silently and looked back across the field towards the Base. It looked quiet enough there in the twilight. Tia could hear no one shouting, only the whisper of the corn stalks touching each other in the breeze. That and the beating of her own heart. The smell of woodsmoke hung on the evening air and mingled with the scent of the dew-dampened earth around them. Rabbit was still listening, his eyes glazed, focused on something in the distance.

"They aren't going to ch-chase us yet," he finally whispered. "But th-they will. You can't run f-f-fast. We b-better hide."

He took her hand and they hurried down the corn rows.

"Where are we going to hide?"

"The old s-strawstack from last year. N-nobody comes around there m-much and th-they're all t-too short to see the top!"

It was almost dark when they reached the straw piles near the cowbarn. Climbing a tree that stood conveniently near the tallest stack, the children crawled out on an overhanging limb and jumped down onto the straw. It was such a pleasant sensation that Tia suddenly realized why the children were forbidden to play there. Even having all that dust go up your nose when you landed didn't keep you from wanting to slide down the pile, climb back up the tree and do it all over again.

Rabbit landed spread-eagle beside her with a whomp. Another dust cloud went up and both of them began to sneeze.

"Ti-ah. . . . Ti-ah?" It was her mother's sharp voice. "Tia! Where are you?"

Both children froze, their index fingers pressed hard against their noses to prevent further sneezing. The call had come from somewhere near the Commons but someone else might be close by. They listened in frightened silence. The voice came again, "Ti-ah?", paused, repeated, "Tia? Answer me!" It was getting closer.

Tia's only response was to begin to stealthily dig her way down into the straw, hollowing out a hole she could hide in. Rabbit, seeing what she was doing, nodded and began to help her. They piled the straw up along the sides of the indentation, burrowed down into it and partially pulled the straw over them as a cover. In the rustle of digging they could hear nothing else, and it was a little while before it was quiet again. Tia noticed the crickets and other night insects had resumed their singing and she relaxed a bit and looked up at the stars.

"Tia?"

The voice came from near the tool shed. The crickets fell silent. Tia felt Rabbit squirm beside her; she reached out as quietly as she could, felt for his hand and squeezed it with a reassurance she did not feel.

"Did you find her?" a male voice called.

"No."

"Well keep hunting, woman. She's your brat and you're responsible. And if that boy's mother was still alive, she'd be answering for him, too."

The children could not tell what was happening; they could only listen to sounds. The church bell tolled five, three times, the signal for everyone to assemble on the Commons. There was some shouting but none of it in distinguishable words. The trees beside them blocked their view of the Base from one side, the barn from the other. Their only direct view was across the fields and they could see nothing there.

The door to the cowbarn was opened and they could see the wavering dim light of a lantern flickering out from the cracks between the boards. Several of the little cows mooed nervously. The light traveled around the barn. One of the Simples, awakened from sleep, yelled out at the intruders and was gruffly told to "Shut up." There was an excited rumble of other Simple voices. Then the light went out, the door was closed and the murmur died away.

They were almost asleep when the death bell began to toll. Startled, Tia turned to find Rabbit looking at her, his face very white in the moonlight. They listened wordlessly as the bell tolled thirty-five times before falling silent.

"I d-d-don't care," whispered Rabbit, "I wa-wa-wanted him to die! Is th-that very bad?"

Tia put her hand over his mouth. "Shhhh. You didn't kill him, silly. He was too big for you to kill."

"I did!" insisted Rabbit, "I th-th-thought 'die!' when he was hitting you—I th-thought it real hard —and th-then his head inside t-t-turned black and he f-f-fell down." His voice was rising and Tia felt his hysteria.

"Shhhh!" hissed Tia. "You can't just wish people dead, Rabbit. You have to hurt them real bad. Then even sometimes they don't die."

"Th-this one d-d-did," whispered Rabbit.

"But not because you wished him dead," she insisted.

"Oh yes!" said Rabbit, nodding with sureness, "She said, 'V-v-varas he's killed'—and I kn-knew he was dead. Don't you remember, I s-s-said th-that's why we had to run?"

"Who said?" thought Tia and she knew the answer.

"The lady in our dream," came the answer from Rabbit. "She said it and she felt scared and, I don't know, kind of really surprised."

It was a moment before she realized he had answered her without speaking. Tia caught her breath in sudden fright. Then it was true! They could talk to each other without words! That was not just a dream. But what was it? And the others —could they hear them, too? She writhed in fear at the thought.

"That's silly," Rabbit's thought was reassuring her. "If they could hear us, they'd know right now where we are. They wouldn't have to hunt for us, would they?" and then, "I'm very tired."

For a moment she had a clear picture of Rabbit's mind replaying the kitchen scene to itself in the cozy darkness of the strawstack. He was trying to understand how he had killed Otto. And wondering what the Major would do to him now. But then she thought of the very real trouble they were in and wished she could escape to the peaceful valley of the Dreams. Beside her Rabbit breathed deeply in sleep.

Ashira's mind linked with hers. First she soothed and when relative calm had been restored to Tia's soul, she asked questions. What had caused Tia's original state of distress? And Rabbit's? Were they being hunted? Why did they find it so difficult to accept the fact of telepathy? Did Tia know who her father was? Tia said they had a lot of Fathers and began to name them. But this wasn't what Ashira wanted to know.

Did her sisters have the same father? This question came from Varas. Tia did not think so but she was not sure. Her mother had never told her which Fathers she had mated with.

At the same time, she was aware that Rabbit was also being questioned. Had he ever wanted to kill before? No. Ashira and Varas seemed pleased to know that. They had become aware of the children's distress due to Ashira's severe and sudden pain when Rabbit was at the peak of his anger. They seemed fascinated with Rabbit and, Tia was not sure what it was, a little wary of him. And she wondered if they truly believed Rabbit could have killed Otto.

"We have very little time." Ashira suddenly brought the questioning session to an end. "You children are in great danger. You must leave your village, and no one must know of your going. You must walk to the west, toward the setting sun. You will find a river—follow it until you reach The Sea. We will find you there. If our maps are reliable, we believe it will be at least a week's journey for the two of you. Take as much food as you can carry. We will be in contact with you whenever you can. We realize what we are asking you to do is dangerous, but we believe you will be in graver danger if you remain where you are. To ask our aid you need not be asleep. This is not a dream but a power with which you are both gifted—another sense, like sight or hearing. To reach us you must picture our faces in your minds."

For the first time Rabbit saw them clearly. Ashira was a tall woman, taller even than Tia. Her hair was dark, her eyes slightly oblique and large. She was dressed in something that looked very clean and around her long neck hung a very pretty stone on a chain. Varas was taller than Ashira; his hair was as white as the woman's gown, but his face looked young. They looked enough alike to be brother and sister.

Beside her Tia felt Rabbit smile to see them and realized she too was pleased by the sight. The children had never known people could look so good.

"Let us see what you look like?" Ashira asked. And the children both tried but somehow they could only project their features in pieces—the shape of a nose, the length of a leg, a mass of hair. "Perhaps, Rabbit, if you would show us how Tia appears to you? And you, Tia, show us Rabbit?"

And then Tia began to giggle to see how tall she seemed to Rabbit, and he was hurt to see that he was so small in her eyes. Each tried to correct the other's image and left Ashira and Varas in a state of confusion.

Ashira dismissed the images in resignation. "When we meet there will be no distortion. Until then, you must use all your courage and intelligence to survive. Can you do it?"

And although neither child was sure what "courage and intelligence" really meant, they agreed to try.

7

She woke up shivering.
It took her some time to realize where she was and
why she was sleeping outside with the open night
sky above her. The straw smelled musty with dew
and where it wasn't warmed by her body, was
damp to the touch. Pieces of straw were poking
into the back of her legs. Rousing herself enough
to scratch, she saw Rabbit was gone. A trail in
the side of the stack showed where he had slid
down to the ground.

She raised her head cautiously and looked over
the top of the stack, hoping to see him coming out
of the bushes by the barn. But he wasn't there.
Thinking where Rabbit could have gone made her
aware that her own bladder was uncomfortably
full. Necessity soon overcame her fear of leaving
the sanctuary of the strawstack and she slid down

the route Rabbit had chosen. Straw tumbled down on top of her and she arose covered with chaff.

"Where could he have gone?" she asked herself as she circled around the grove of willows behind the barn. It was risky to get too close to the barn. The Simples might be awake and looking out.

"Food." The answer entered her mind and she wasn't sure if it was her thought or Rabbit's. Then she received an image of Rabbit tugging open the door to the root cellar and this time she knew he was telling her what he was doing. "Stay there," he warned her. "I have a sack. I can carry a lot."

Ill at ease, she walked back to the strawstack and waited for him. The sky in the east was beginning to lighten. If Rabbit didn't come back soon, she would have to hide somewhere else. The women would be coming out to the fields in an hour.

"Tia! Hide!"

She didn't know why but the urgency in the message was unmistakable. But where to hide? If she had to run, the strawstack was too exposed. She would be seen and caught immediately. Without any plan in mind except staying under cover, she took off through the trees, keeping to the denser growth around the fringe of the settlement.

It was hard to see where she was going in the

darkness and she almost fell several times over vines and rocks. She tried to get Rabbit to answer her thoughts but there was no response. Mosquitoes swarmed over the thickets, and Tia had to keep brushing them off her arms and legs as she stumbled along. It occurred to her that anyone who was up and out could hear her crashing about; she tried to walk more quietly. Her nose told her she was approaching the back of the new garbage pit and latrine area and she hurried faster again to get away from the odor.

The big root cellar was on the other side of the settlement near the smokehouse and game-dressing sheds. Part of the ancient structure of the Base, its cement floor had been lined with clean sand, its top roofed with timbers and covered with earth until now it looked like a big grassy mound. A well-worn path through the grass led to its heavy wooden door.

By the time Tia reached the woods behind the smokehouse, it was almost daylight. She could see smoke coming from the messhall chimney and wondered who was taking Father Otto's place in the kitchen this morning. Then she remembered her gold ring and wondered who had it now. Probably the Major; he usually took all the pretty things people found. She felt no remorse about

Otto's death, only resentment that he had deprived her of something she felt to be rightfully hers.

It was then that she noticed a figure standing outside the door to the root cellar. She stopped still. It was a soldier. In his hand he was swinging the heavy club of a sentry. Very cautiously she crept behind the trunk of the nearest big tree and watched. The man stood quietly, apparently listening. The bell rang for breakfast and he looked over in the direction of the messhall, then began to pace impatiently. But he did not leave the door.

"Why he's guarding something!" Tia thought to herself, and then realized, "He's guarding Rabbit!" When the first panic had passed she tried to concentrate very hard on Rabbit, calling his name over and over to herself and she finally received a shamed and tearful image. But the little boy was too upset to respond coherently. He had failed, he thought, failed before they started and now he was trapped alone there in the dark of the cellar. He was afraid of something she could not hope to understand.

Feeling his despair, Tia nearly cried herself. It was so hopeless. They might as well give up now. They would be punished, she knew, or at least she was sure she would be punished. She speculated on what the punishment might be—whipping? Probably. But it would depend on what the Major decided the worst crime was—her having the gold ring, or telling the Fathers "no," or fighting with Father Otto. They couldn't blame her and Rabbit for Otto's dying, she reasoned, but they must think it was really bad or they wouldn't have locked up Rabbit.

A second soldier came running up the path toward the cellar.

"Major says I'm to relieve you while you go eat. You seen any sign of the witch yet?"

"Nah. What you expect they'll do to her when we get her?"

"What do you think? Major wants her dead. You got to admit, it won't be much of a loss."

The sentry snorted a laugh of agreement. "Still, I hope I don't have to be the one to do it. Killing kids—even that girl—ain't my idea of man's work."

"Major and Karl say she killed Otto."

"If you ask me, Otto died of fat. He got real mad and burst something in that fat gut of his."

"Major and Karl was right there. They saw her do it!" the soldier insisted, "She bit him and he dropped dead of it!"

"Yeah, sure," the sentry scoffed. "I believe that like I believed Rabbit when he said he done it.

What's for breakfast?"

Tia clutched the tree to keep from falling. The shock of their words made her sick to her stomach. They were going to kill her! She couldn't really believe it—and yet some still center of her mind told her it was true. She knew some children died; she had seen two little boys buried only the year before. But they had died because they were sick, not because anyone killed them.

She slipped to the ground and sat with her arms wrapped around her knees—hunched up, head down—and wondered how they would kill her. Clubs? Hanging? The thought would not bear holding and she broke off and stared at an ant hill near her feet, the ants busily going about their jobs of carrying sand grains. If she moved her foot she could squash them all, destroy their home. But she didn't.

She was still sitting that way an hour later, staring dully at the ground, when the church bell began to toll for a burial service. When it finished ringing she rose to her feet, brushed the dirt off her dress and stretched. She might be friendless, alone, and a wanted criminal—all that could not be changed now. She was still free, she was alive and she was hungry.

The settlement seemed to be silent. Except for

the guard at the root cellar door, she could see no one about. They were probably out burying Otto. She thought of the roast rabbit of the night before and salivated. But trying to go to the messhall was out of the question. She would be spotted by the guard before she passed the second building. Then she remembered the smokehouse and the long rows of smoked rabbits and squirrels hanging from its beams. If she could get in from the back, the guard couldn't see her.

Noiselessly she made her way through the underbrush to the rear of the smokehouse. The building sat on a stone foundation, one stone of which could be rolled back to allow a hungry child to enter. It had not been designed that way purposely but the children had adapted it to their needs. She crept up through the weeds at the edge of the clearing and paused to listen. There was no sound. Then with the courage born of despair, she crawled into the clearing around the back of the house, tugged the stone sideways, slipped through the opening into the aromatic dimness of the building, and pulled the stone back into position from the inside.

It took her eyes a moment to adjust from the bright morning sunshine to the darkness of the windowless smokehouse. She knelt there, listening

to see if the guard had heard the clink of the rolling stone. When she felt fairly sure he had not,
she turned her full attention to the meat hanging
above her.

Brace upon brace, the salt-rimed carcasses hung
from the rafters; in that corner, squirrel, in the
other woodmice, and directly above her, row after
row of rabbit. Tia liked the most deeply-cured
meat best. That hung from the hooks in the attic.
Silently she climbed the wall ladder up and
through the hole in the rafters. Stepping carefully over the widely spaced boards she chose a
brace of small rabbits, untied it from the string,
and carried it over to the darkest corner of the
cramped space. There, above the door below, the
attic floor was solid and she could sit in comfort.

Sensing she would need the energy she ate a
whole rabbit, and when she had eaten, she began
to feel much better. Now that the initial shock had
passed, she could think clearly again. Her first
idea was to call Ashira—but shyness mixed with
doubts kept her from trying that. Even if she were
real, what could she do from far away? But, she
thought to herself, if they want to kill me, they'll
have to catch me first. Rabbit and I got away from
them—Rabbit! She had forgotten about him.
There had to be a way to get him free!

Little beams of sunlight poured onto the floor around her from chinks in the wall between the logs. She crawled over to a chink and pressed her eye to it. She could see the root cellar, the path and part of the square from here. The discovery cheered her for no logical reason. Looking at the door of the cellar, she thought "Rabbit?—Are you there?—Rabbit?" And when he didn't respond, she became angry. "Rabbit, you answer me and right now!"

"What?" The first impression was one of sullenness and fear.

"Are you O.K.?"

"It's dark down here."

"I'm going to get you out."

She felt him brighten with hope, then the hope was clouded over by depression. "You can't. There's a sentry in front of the door. I called and called to him and he just laughed. He won't let me out even if you ask him nice."

"Rabbit, you listen to me! I'm going to get you out. I haven't figured out how yet, but I'm going to do it. Ashira told us to take care of each other."

"She doesn't care. She's just in our dreams. I tried to get her and she didn't answer. She's just dumb baby stuff!"

She could feel him begin to cry again.

"Rabbit, stop that! It won't help us."

"Nothing will help—they want to kill you because they think. . . ."

"I know. I heard the guards talking. I'm going to run away."

"You c-c-can't l-l-leave me here!" He wailed this aloud in his distress.

"Shut up, kid!" yelled the guard. "You think I like keeping a kid shut up down there? I got my orders from the Major. So just shut up. Yelling won't help you."

It took some time before he was calm enough to receive her again. "I won't leave without getting you out," she promised. "But you must be quiet. While you're waiting, stuff all the dried apples you can find into your sack—the sliced ones —you can fit more in that way. I can't get you out before dark, so don't get worried. They'll probably feed you sometime during the day. Eat as much as you can, O.K.? Now I have to be quiet and think. When you want me, think about me hard like you did before."

Tia's planning session was distracted by several incidents during the day. Once the Major and some other Fathers came to the cellar to question the boy on her whereabouts. She saw Rabbit hauled out of the darkness by the back of his shirt to stand small and blinking in the sun. He told them repeatedly, and truthfully, that he didn't know where she was hiding. Just as repeatedly the Major slapped his face.

Anna brought him a plate of food at dinnertime and scolded the guard for keeping a child in the dark. Later the hunters trooped past to report they had found where the witch had been hiding in the strawstack, but she was gone. They had searched all the buildings where she could hide.

At nightfall, her plans desperate but complete, Tia ate part of the second rabbit. The sentry was replaced by another after supper. She waited until it was almost dark but still light enough to see her way across the open spaces in the floor, then crept down the ladder. When several hours passed and she could hear no more noises from the settlement, she crept out the way she had entered. Before she left, she carefully placed two braces of smoked rabbit on the floor near the escape hole where they could easily be reached.

When she was deep enough into the surrounding woods, she began to run, partially to escape the mosquitoes and partially from tension from being so inactive all day. Her route took her around the settlement until she was over near the women's house. Staying close to the buildings, she hurried over the grass toward the messhall kitchen. She was surprised to see the kitchen door open. Someone had been left on guard there. For a moment her plans faltered, but then she shrugged to herself. She had nothing to lose.

Standing well back from the door she looked into the kitchen. It seemed empty. Then she noticed a figure on the bench near the fireplace. It was Anna—and she was asleep. Tia sighed with relief. Making sure no one else was about, she crept into the room and silently picked up a small kettle and spoon from the pile on the shelf. Going on tiptoe to the fireplace, she stooped and spooned glowing coals into the kettle and just as silently left.

At the schoolhouse she hurriedly stuffed the kettle with dry weeds and grasses. As it licked into flame she shoved the whole thing beneath the porch of the building. Waiting only long enough to see that the dry floorboards were beginning to glow in the dark, she ran for the cover of the trees.

By the time she reached the root cellar, flames from the roof of the school could be seen across the village. She heard the guard yell and then saw him run toward the fire. It took her only a few minutes to reach the cellar door, lift the bolt and pull the door open—but it seemed an unbearably long time.

"Hurry!" she hissed to the sleepy Rabbit as he stumbled up the incline, dragging the foodbag in the dust. As she grabbed his hand to guide him, they heard the church bell begin to ring a fire alarm.

"Wh-wh-what's that?" he asked. Tia was carefully closing the door and replacing the bolt.

"Shhh—we've got to be quiet. They might come back. Hurry!" She pulled the groggy boy around behind the smokehouse, shoved the stone aside, reached in and grabbed the rabbits.

"W-w-will that be enough?" he whispered when he saw them.

"It has to be. I don't have time for more." She looked him squarely in the face. "You might be safer here, Rabbit. If you go with me now—well—they want to kill me. . . ."

"D-d-don't be s-silly," he interrupted. "We d-don't have the time."

8

Away from the village the trees grew taller, the underbrush thinned and the children could make better time in the darkness. Tia was leading them towards the hills where she played on Sunday. A quarter of a mile beyond was the Path, a wide, graded cut stretching for miles through the wooded uplands. Tia had never followed the Path for any great distance. It lay too far from the Base for her to explore to her satisfaction and still return home in time for worship. But as she had made her escape plans that afternoon, it seemed to her the only route she could think of that would lead her away without getting lost in the woods.

"Do you th-think we-we can make it?" whispered Rabbit after they had been walking for an hour.

"We have to now, don't we?"

"B-but can we? We're pretty li-little—and it m-might be f-far."

"I'm as big as any grownup and you're as smart."

Rabbit thought that over. "Th-h-that's true!" he said finally and with great satisfaction. "B-but what if they ch-chase us? You c-can't run very f-fast long."

"We'll just have to make sure they never see us, Rabbit. We'll walk at night and hide and sleep when the sun is out so we stay warm. And maybe they won't chase us. They might miss you, but they'll be just as glad I'm gone."

"Your m-m-mother might m-miss you—and if I was still th-there—I'd m-miss you," Rabbit said loyally.

Tia thought of her mother and of the relief her disappearance would be to the woman and to her half-sisters. Then she dismissed the thought; there was no time now for self-pity. "We'd better not talk any more," she said. "We'd better save our breath for walking. If we have to talk, we can try think-talking like we did before. We might have to be very quiet before we get where we're going."

"O.K." agreed Rabbit happily, his self-confidence restored by freedom.

When they reached the base of the hills, they rested and listened to see if they were being followed. They could hear nothing but the sounds of the woods around them, insects singing, an occasional twig snapping as a small animal moved in the night, the winds that sporadically blew through the trees.

They found the Path easily in the dark, and once up the embankment, walking was much easier since nothing grew up there but poverty grass and wild mustard. Overhead the moon was so bright it dimmed the starshine. They walked on long after they were tired, driven by fear and the still present threat of capture. In many places on the Path the poverty grass was blown flat by the wind and made a smooth carpet for their tired feet. And although they didn't realize it at the time, its flatness obscured their trail.

The meat Tia carried grew very heavy after a time and she felt as though she were walking along in her sleep. Rabbit sometimes stumbled now as he walked beside her, and she shifted the meat to her other shoulder and took his hand to guide him. After a time the sleepiness seemed to pass and they walked on more easily. But finally Rabbit tripped over a vine and fell, nearly pulling her down on top of him.

"Come on," Tia said as she pushed herself to her feet. "It's still dark. We can't stop yet. We've got to go on!"

"I d-d-don't think I can go much f-f-further."

Tia felt her head swimming with fatigue as she pulled him to his feet. The effort of partially lifting his weight made her knees quiver.

"Well," she said, accepting the inevitable, "we can't sleep here. Let's find a place to hide."

They slid down the embankment on their grass-smoothed soles and found themselves in an area of dense underbrush. They walked along beside it for a time, grateful for the breeze that kept the mosquitoes away from them. When an opening appeared in the bushes, Rabbit automatically pulled away from her and headed into the trees. She followed. In the leaf-filled hollow of an uprooted oak they curled up to sleep, spoon-fashion to keep warm, and not even the mosquitoes could wake them until the sun was far past noon.

When Tia opened her eyes she saw Rabbit sitting cross-legged beside her, eating. In his right fist he clutched a big chunk of meat; his left was bulging with slices of dried apple. Like a small animal that feels no threat, he was totally intent on feeding. As full consciousness returned, she found her left arm was numb from lying on it; there was a stone pressing into her hip bone, and she itched all over from mosquito bites. She rolled over onto her back and put an arm across her face to cover her eyes from the sun.

"You s-s-sure sleep a long time," Rabbit greeted her. "I got hungry and it woke me up. You hungry?" He held out a chunk of the grayish meat.

"Yeah." Tia sat up. "Wait till I brush off." Damp leaves clung to her bare arms, leaf bits were tangled in her hair. An enterprising inchworm was measuring her bare knee. She flicked the poor worm halfway across the little hollow and then proceeded to tidy herself as best she could before taking the meat her friend offered. She ate quickly and in silence, still half asleep. The meat tasted salty to her, but good. The apple chips were rubbery and almost tasteless.

"I wish we had some water."

"Th-there's a p-pool down that way," Rabbit pointed into the woods. "I was l-looking around while you slept. It's not far. Want to go?"

She nodded, shoved the last of her meat into her mouth and stood up. She put the remains of the smoked rabbit into the apple sack. Rabbit carefully buried the bones under a pile of leaves at the base of the tree and then looked around to make sure there was no trace left of their having rested here. The area met with his satisfaction and they set off to get a drink.

Rabbit's pool filled a deep depression in the woods. At one side of it was a rock pile covered with briars. The water was still and tasted of the earth and leaves. Tia lay flat on her stomach and drank.

"B-b-boy! you really were dry!"

A branch cracked sharply somewhere in the direction they had just come from. The children looked at each other in alarm. They were being followed! There was only the rock pile to hide behind—the sound was too close to try running. They crouched behind the stones.

There was the sucking sound of feet pulling out of thick mud, then the sound of something drinking, followed by more squelching in the mud. Tia looked at Rabbit. That didn't sound like a person! And yet . . . ? They were ready to bolt when they heard a gruff, fleshy "snort!-snore-snort!" followed by a vigorous sniff. Tia raised her head cautiously and looked through the tangle of briars.

At the edge of the pool stood a big white animal with no hair, floppy pointed ears, a flat wet pink nose covered with mud, and small squinty eyes that seemed to be looking right at her with such intelligence and curiosity that she gasped in surprise.

"Wh-what is it?" Rabbit scrambled to his feet and looked.

"I don't know," whispered Tia. "Do you think it's some kind of cow?"

"It's about as b-big—but—it doesn't look like one."

Just then the animal gave a threatening grunt and was answered by a sharp squeal from the reeds behind it. The children saw that it was accompanied by three small animals just like itself.

"It's got babies!"

"L-look at their n-noses!"

At the repeated sound of their voices, the animal backed out of the mud, gave a grunting command, wheeled to the right and trotted off into the trees, followed by her hurrying brood.

"She heard us."

"W-we didn't say anything b-bad. Wh-why did she get scared?"

Tia didn't answer. She was thinking. It had never occurred to her that there were any animals other than those she knew; rabbits, squirrels, and mice in the woods, and the little cows they raised at the Base. The Major always said in his sermons that all the other animals, and something called "birds" had died along with all the people that used to live here a long time ago. There were fish that lived in water like frogs, but it was forbidden to eat those. Tia was just as glad, because they were pretty and silver-looking, not like something you ate at all. But if there were other animals . . . and they came this close to the Base. . . .? They could be caught and raised and eaten . . . and the women and hunters wouldn't have to work so hard for food. Anna had said once that they didn't have cows when she was a girl—Tia thought she was so old she'd just forgotten about them. . . .

"Why haven't the hunters seen these animals?" she suddenly asked Rabbit.

"M-maybe they have?"

"Then why don't they ever catch them?"

"M-maybe they're too big—m-maybe they're afraid of them?"

"Maybe." But Tia didn't believe it. The Fathers had lied. For some reason they wanted the people to work very hard. Why?

"We b-better go." Rabbit picked up the sack and started off toward the path. Tia followed, trying to walk as quietly as he did and almost succeeding, her mind full of new thoughts.

It was late afternoon when they reached the bank of the Path again. They followed it cautiously from the protection of the woods for half a mile or more and then, when they were sure it was safe, climbed the embankment and walked along at a faster pace. They talked little as they walked, having little to say. At intervals they took turns carrying the food bag. It was almost sunset when Tia stopped and caught Rabbit by the arm.

"Smell!" came her thought to him.

His round head went up and his small nostrils flared as he repeatedly wrinkled his nose.

"Smoke." He verified her thought.

They were down the embankment and into the bushes in less than a second. There they paused and listened. They could hear no sounds of man, but, Tia spotted a thin gray spiral of smoke rising against the red clouds of the sunset. It was to their right, west of them, and seemed to be burning on the Path.

"Sneak like me," Rabbit commanded as he started off in the direction of the smoke.

"Why are you going there?"

"We've got to see who it is. Maybe it's someone after us—or maybe it's just some of the hunters following their snare lines and they don't know about us yet. If it's just hunters, we don't have to be so scared. But if it's not. . . ."

"What if they hear us?"

"They won't—not if we sneak good," Rabbit assured her.

"Let's wait until it's darker."

It was almost night when the children crept close enough to see the fire. They circled around it among the trees, keeping far enough away not to be heard or seen. But that meant they could not clearly see who was sitting there beside it.

"You stay here," Rabbit told Tia. "I'm a better sneak than you. I'm going close enough to hear."

"What if they catch you?"

"They won't. And even if they do, they won't hurt me." The trouble with thought communication was that Rabbit couldn't keep unpleasant things from showing, so Tia knew the rest of his thought—"but they might kill you."

It was a very effective thought, one she had forgotten since the terror of the night before. She watched Rabbit slink off into the gloom of the underbrush and found that if she took her eyes away from him for a moment, she had difficulty spotting him again, so well did he blend into the darkness of the woods.

"It's not just hunters," came his report a few minutes later. "It's hunters and soldiers. . . ." She felt his sudden thrill of recognition and fear. Had they caught him? "They can't see me." He answered her frantic question. "The Major is here! You have to quit talking to me now because I can't tell you things in my head and listen to them at the same time."

It seemed like hours that she waited for Rabbit to come back, although it was less than half an hour before he signaled her, "Don't get scared, I'm almost there." He stepped out of the bushes beside her, his finger over his lips as a sign to be silent. "We'd better get away from here fast. I'll tell you what I found out when we're in a safer place."

He led the way through the trees, his eyes being better than hers in the darkness. When they reached a point he felt was sufficiently far from the encampment, he detoured back to the Path and they hurried along in the moonlight, intent only on escape. It was almost midnight when they stopped to rest and eat. By agreement now they would do no more talking "aloud"—only mind-talking. Tia broke the last of the first dried rabbit in two and handed the larger piece to Rabbit. Each took a fistful of apples and settled down to eat.

"Now tell me?" she asked.

"There's seven of them—the Major, three hunters and three soldiers. They're carrying lots of stuff, as if they might be gone a long time."

"Why the Major—why does he care? He never leaves the Base."

"I don't know. They haven't found our tracks yet because the Major said we had to be somewhere near the Base, that we were too dumb to live long in the woods. But a hunter said if he was running away, he'd take the easy way and that was the Path. And the Major said then why hadn't they seen us, and the hunter said because we had a good start. The Major said he hoped the hunter was right—it's Ed, you know?—the mean one that likes to kill rabbits with his hands and laughs so funny? He said the Major would get his chance to see if you really are a witch, and the Major said he knew what you were. Then Ed said something about if he wanted you caught to just trust him as a guide and the Major said it wasn't trust he cared about but discipline and you were to be made an example of something—I forget what. Hey, he said you burned down the school—you never told me that!"

"I had to get them away from the door so I could get you out."

Rabbit grinned with pleasure at the thought of

the school burning. "I bet Father Neal was mad!"

"What else did they say? Where are they going tomorrow?"

"I think they're going to follow the Path some more. The Major said they would have to go to sleep because he wanted to start as soon as it was light. Oh yeah, one of them said there was a river ahead and then high hills and he had never gone beyond the river."

"Why not?"

"He didn't say."

Tia withdrew into private thought. If the men stayed on the Path, then no matter how fast she and Rabbit walked at night, the men would catch up to them during the day. If they left the Path, she was afraid the two of them would get lost before the night was out and wander aimlessly. She swallowed nervously and remembered she was thirsty. They would need water and food; the smoked meat and apples would only last another two days, even if they didn't eat very much. And walking made them extra hungry.

"I'm going to try to 'see' Ashira."

Rabbit nodded agreement but didn't look too hopeful about it. His experience in the root cellar had quickly dimmed his new faith.

Tia's mind reached for a view of the valley with

its gaily colored houses and white-sailed windmills. There was no answering thought and the
girl was not sure if she was seeing the place or only
remembering it from her dreams. She tried to
visualize Ashira's face and then, remembering
their last contact, she thought of the Gyrestone,
imagining she could see its center with the waves
of blue surrounding it.

Ashira's mind answered so forcefully the girl
almost cried out with surprise.

"Where are you?" the woman wanted to know.
"Varas and I have been trying to reach you—
where is Rabbit?"

As if Ashira were there to see, Tia reached out
and touched Rabbit, then, remembering, opened
her mind to him so that he could join the conversation. Both of them together began to relate their
flight and pursuit with such excitement that
Ashira had to ask them to either take turns or slow
down. Rabbit immediately wanted to know why
she hadn't answered him when he needed her in
the cellar. She said that she had not received his
distress; that there was still a limit to his transmission and reception range, but she strongly suspected that would improve with training.

But as neither child knew what she meant,
Ashira quickly returned to their present situation.

Learning that, she became distressed before she could hide the fact from them. Varas was called and joined her.

As Tia had suspected, there was little the two could do to protect them. They had expected the children to carry more food with them from the Base than they had and seemed alarmed to know the actual conditions now.

Ashira showed them various plants and berries they could eat should they find them. Varas showed them puffballs and oyster mushrooms that grew from fallen trees. How near were they to the river? Rabbit told them what the hunter had said. Varas showed them what shellfish looked like, and fish, and then tried to convince them that such things could be eaten.

But they were on their way to find them! The children received an image of the ship with its solar sails up. If the maps could still be trusted, the weather counted on, they would reach the coast of the children's land in about ten days. Then it would be a matter of locating two children in the wilderness or along the shore, if the children made good time.

"And now it is time for you to continue," Ashira decided. "Stay on your path for the night. Do not use speech—your voices will carry. Avoid any high grass—footsteps in high grass can be seen in the morning light—even in moonlight. Hide before dawn and contact us then before you sleep."

"Why can't we talk to you in our Dreams like always?" Tia asked.

"Because you need rest, and contact takes valuable energy. And also because we want you to become adept at consciously calling us so you may begin to learn the extent and control of your powers."

That reminded Rabbit of something. "Did I really kill Father Otto? Tia doesn't believe me. And the guard just laughed at me when I told him I'd done it . . . so I didn't tell anyone else. Did I do it?"

There was a deliberate hesitation from Ashira before she finally replied, "Yes, Rabbit. You did."

Her obvious regret at having to confirm this fact to him made Rabbit flush with shame. "Do you think I'm bad? He said he was going to kill Tia—he called her 'witch' and he hit her hard and . . ."

"Rabbit!" Her mind momentarily seized control of his to block the memory and reassure him. What she wanted him to understand about his unique capability would take months of teaching; there was no time for it now. "You had no way of knowing then what would happen, Rabbit, but I want you to promise me you will not deliberately wish anyone else dead."

"Even if they catch us?"

"Even then."

"O.K." He promised sincerely, not understanding why she asked this of him, but wanting her to be his friend. And Ashira knew this.

"When we meet, little one, we will teach you to understand."

"There is no time to discuss the irrevocable," Varas interrupted. "The children must continue— and they must believe we will find them. The farther away they are from those men, the safer they will be."

9

It began to rain towards morning, a chilling summer rain. Tia and Rabbit stumbled on, blinking their eyes against the drops, tripping over vines growing across the Path. When it became light enough to see where they were, the woods looked no different than the place they had stopped the day before. They were so tired and wet it made little difference to them where they hid, as long as it was dry. But dryness was a luxury hard to find and they wandered about among the trees until daylight, getting farther and farther away from the Path.

"What is that?" Rabbit was listening. Away to the north came the faint sound of water rushing over a gravel bottom. That sound, along with the splat of rain on the leaves over them, made Tia shiver uncontrollably. "Let's go see!" and without waiting for her answer, he was off.

"But what about the Major?" Tia thought to him.

"It's raining on them, too. It'll take them a long time to catch up with us."

Tia caught up with Rabbit at the edge of the river bend. Wide and shallow, the river flowed down from the hills to the northeast and seemed to make an abrupt turn west at the point where they stood. There were large square stones at intervals in the riverbed as if to guide it around the curve. Sandbars stretched out into the channel. While Tia was still drinking Rabbit started towards one of these.

"Stop!" came Tia's order. "You'll leave tracks in the sand."

Rabbit looked back at her, chagrined but knowing she was right.

"Let's hunt for rocks." She began to walk along the bank, heading west by habit. Away from the bend, the river narrowed and deepened again for many hundreds of yards before running across an outcropping of stone. Here the children crossed and entered the woods on the other side. And somehow, having the river between themselves and their pursuers, they felt safer. Still following the rock outcropping, they found a small over-hanging ledge and, beneath it, a shallow cave half hidden by brush. Its bottom was full of windswept dead leaves and smaller brush. After cleaning out the roughest of the debris, the two of them huddled together and went to sleep.

Sometime in midafternoon they were awakened by a shout. They lay very still, listening to the thudding of their hearts and not daring to breathe. There was an answering shout from the distance.

"Over here!" a man's voice called.

They had been found. Tia closed her eyes in resignation and despair.

"Any tracks?"

"Not yet."

Hope glimmered faintly within her, then died with the next call.

"They headed this way when they left the Path —you sure they crossed over here?"

The answer was unintelligible. They heard nothing more for a few minutes and then they heard both men talking. The one across the river had joined his companion on their side.

"You find anything over here?"

"No," admitted the other, "but they must have crossed over. I saw where they went down the bank from the Path through the creepers—and there were tracks in the dirt around a groundhog hole. They moved around a lot, but they were heading in this general direction."

"The two of them still together?"

"Yeah."

"You think we should go get the Major and the rest?"

"Yeah. There's a big cave down here a ways. Big enough to light a fire and dry out for the night."

"You think he's going to want to stop early if they're around here?"

"He might not like it, but he'll do what we say. If we left him out here he'd be lost in an hour and he knows that."

"You want to keep on looking while I get them others—or you want me to hunt and you get them?"

"I'll hunt."

"You think they're in the cave, Ed?"

"Yeah, it would be a good place to hide."

"How would they know about it?"

"They don't have to know about it, stupid. Any dumb animal knows enough to get in out of the rain."

"They don't know we're in here!" Rabbit's triumphant deduction almost gave Tia a headache. "They think we're in some other bigger cave!"

"Not a sound," she warned him.

"I won't," he promised, "but boy!, isn't it lucky we didn't find that other place! I wonder how far away it is?"

The bushes at the cave mouth whisked as someone brushed them in passing. Tia raised her head quietly and saw the heavily muscled legs of a man standing less then ten feet away. He paused and half turned, then continued on, heading back towards the river. Although they lay very still and listened, they could not tell where the other man was.

"We might as well go back to sleep," Tia finally told Rabbit. "If they find us, there's nothing we can do about it. If they don't, we'll need the rest."

"I don't think I can sleep any more," answered Rabbit. "I'm too scared." But the quiet continued and after a bit Tia saw his eyelids drooping. He fell asleep before she did.

It was dark again when she woke up. Rabbit stirred restlessly beside her and she put out her hand to quiet him.

"Are you awake?" he asked. And learning she was, "I thought of something!" and he related a plan. It seemed risky but she agreed it was worth trying.

Leaving their food sack behind, they crawled to the entrance of their little cave and listened.

They could hear nothing but the sound of the per-
sistent rain on the leaves around them. High overhead the wind was scudding clouds along, occasionally revealing a few stars only to cover them
up again. The woods sighed in a sudden gust of
wind and for a few minutes the rain fell harder
and then returned to a drizzle. In the moment following the wind gust they saw a flickering glow of
light glisten on the wet tree trunks to the north and
knew then where their pursuers were camped.

Like shadows they slipped from the cave mouth,
picked their way along the rain-slick rocks to the
forest floor and disappeared into the protective
covering of the trees, heading for the river. Dark
as it was, the river was easy to find; it seemed
louder now than before. Reaching the banks they
deliberately walked in the rain-soaked mud and
sand along the narrow shore until they came to the
bend. Here the sandbars gleamed faintly white in
the darkness. Leading the way, Tia chose the
deepest sandbanks, those free of all gravel, and the
two of them started to cross to the other side.

Water was beginning to cover some of the banks
and, by the time they reached the stream's centre,
came up to Tia's waist. Hearing a muffled cry
from Rabbit, she turned to see him up to his arm-
pits in the cold water and very nearly lifted off

his feet by the current. Grabbing his hand, she tugged him after her into the shallow water of the next sandbar, and from there they made their way to the opposite bank by leaping from bar to bar.

Carefully leaving signs of their passing, they walked back to the Path and up and along it until they thought they were close to the rapids that led to their cave. Choosing a patch of soaking grass not blown down by the wind, they deliberately tramped out a ring covering the width of the path, then quartered it with lines that led down the embankment on both sides.

Rabbit was so pleased with that touch that Tia could hear him chuckling to himself as he sloughed through the grass, mashing it down so that only a blind man could miss seeing it in the morning. When they had tramped the ring and cross bars flat enough so they could see it in the dark, they made their way back down to the river.

It was more difficult crossing back over the rocks at night; while Tia held onto his hand so that she might pull him out if he slipped into deep spots, Rabbit felt their way across literally foot by foot. Trying to find the cave mouth in the darkness was even harder. They missed it three times before locating the brush pile shielding its entrance.

Safe inside and too excited to mind that they were again soaking wet and very cold, Rabbit said, "They're going to go crazy trying to find which way we went!"

But the more Tia thought about the ring in the grass, the more it worried her. "Wouldn't it have been better just to make one path? One going off on the other side?"

"No, now they're going to wonder why we were playing games on the path—they'll follow our tracks down to the river and across the sandbars and over to the other side—and then they'll find the ring! It'll drive them crazy!"

"Yes—but will it fool them?"

"They think we're on this side of the river now —but after they see the tracks, they'll know we've gone back across and don't realize we're being chased—and things like that. . . ?"

"I hope so," thought Tia, but she was worried.

"Let's eat?" suggested Rabbit.

10

They heard the men leave in the early morning, heard their excited shouts as they found the footprints. Now came the hardest part, waiting to see if the ruse worked or the hunters would come back. For hours they huddled there, cramped and chilled in the little cave, listening for any sound other than insects and the rain. None came. Finally Rabbit could bear the silence no longer.

"C-c-can we talk?" he whispered. "I'm g-getting kind of lonely j-just th-thinking to you."

"O.K.—but just whispers."

"Wh-when do you th-think the rain will stop?" Tia shrugged.

"D-do you think we c-can go soon?"

"We'd better wait until dark."

"B-but we don't s-see anything that way. I li-li-like to explore!"

"Me, too. But Ashira told us to walk at night so they can't see us."

"Maybe sh-she's explored a whole lot more th-than we have. She's p-pretty grown-up, you know."

"Maybe. But I don't think she even thought of exploring. I don't think she thinks anything around here is worth exploring. The first time I dreamed of their place I saw her tell Varas I was coming in from deadlands."

"W-we're not dead," puzzled Rabbit, and then, his mind flitting to another thought, "Do you miss your treasures?"

"I forgot about them," Tia said truthfully, and now that she remembered, they seemed important a long time ago, when she was a child. In fact, everything seemed a long time ago. "What I miss is my bed at night."

"M-me, too—I liked to hear the straw rustle under the covers. Wh-when I was little, I used to pre-pretend I was a cow—and curl up with my legs under me because it rustled more that w-way. Cows always l-look so c-comfortable! Father N-neal hit me when he saw me sleeping that way."

"Why?"

"He d-d-didn't say—he n-never says why he hits

you mostly. He j-j-just hits. So I don't sleep that
way anymore."

"I always used to go to sleep imagining I had a
friend, somebody who thought like I did, someone
to curl up against . . . but that was when I was
very little . . ." She stopped and blushed, embarrassed by her self-betrayal.

"D-don't feel b-bad about that, Tia, because I
s-s-still feel th-that way—th-that's why I like having you for a fr-friend. We m-might be in trouble
—but at l-least we're not lonesome."

He crawled up to the cave mouth and looked
out cautiously for a long time, then turned around.
"Let's go, Tia—please? I th-think they've g-gone
on ahead on the Path. Otherwise they'd be b-back
by n-now."

The logic of it appealed to her almost as much
as the wish to get out of the dark cave. "O.K." she
said, "but we must be very careful." She picked
up the empty food sack and thriftily tied its draw-
cords around her waist, then crawled out of the
cave after him.

The rain had lessened and the sky was lighter.

"Wh-which way are w-we going to go?"

"Along the riverbank, I guess. That's west and
there are trees to hide behind if we have to."

"O.K."

They started off again, cautious at first but soon relaxing when it appeared no one else was nearby. The river had risen from the long rain and rushed along beside them, brown and frothy where there were rocks in the stream bed. They walked for several hours before it occurred to them that they were very hungry and they had nothing to eat.

"L-let's see if we can find some of those th-things Varas said might be in the river?" he suggested.

Tia looked down at the water. "I don't think you can see them until it settles down."

"I c-can f-f-feel them."

Rabbit slid down the bank and gingerly stuck a bare foot into the water. "Nothing but little stones here," he reported. Hunching down he reached in with a paw and pulled out a handful of gravel, looked at it carefully and then let it dribble through his fingers back into the water. "M-maybe they're deeper in the water?" he said and began to wade in.

"Don't, Rabbit!" For some reason Tia was scared.

"It's O.K. It f-feels good and cool. Why don't you come in and c-cool off and get clean?"

Tia looked at her arms, covered with mosquito bites. The rain had made light spots all over them and small rivulets ran down from her wrists to her elbows. As she stood there hesitating, her legs began to itch as they dried in the breeze. Rabbit was right; it would be nice to wash. She waded in after him. Picking up sand she scoured her arms and legs as she had been taught to do when bathing. She dunked her head under and washed the accumulation of weed seeds, dust, chaff and bits of leaves from her tangle of hair. Seeing she was washing her head, Rabbit decided to help her by splashing handfuls of water at her and soon the bath had turned into a water fight.

"Hey," yelled Rabbit, "this is j-j-just like when I was l-little. It's f-f-fun!" and then "Ulp!" as Tia hit him square in the mouth with a palmful of water. He ducked and splattered back at her with both hands. "How come they don't let us p-play once we mm-move out of the Infant House?"

"Who knows?" giggled Tia, and threw more water in his face.

His spitting instigated a new game, seeing how much water they could take in their mouths and how accurately they could spit it at the other's face. But that palled quickly. It was too hard for Tia to breathe and spit, too. Rabbit won all the time.

As she rested, her glance fell on a small branch

floating past. She reached out and grabbed it. "Here—catch!" she called and tossed it to Rabbit who fell backward into the water in his too quick effort to obey.

Tia watched him swim after the stick and envied his grace in the water. She was a poor swimmer under optimum conditions, and the strong current here in this small river made her uneasy. The only place she swam with any feeling of security was in the cows' watering pond.

With the stick grasped firmly in his hand, Rabbit swam back towards her and took up a position about ten feet away along the bank. With an effort too obviously intended to make her feel over-confident, he tossed Tia three easy throws. She returned each in the same manner, waiting to see when he was going to zing it to her and laughing at the all-too-innocent look on his face.

When the zinger came on the fourth throw it was a high, arcing end-over-end toss. She turned and ran through the shallows, neck twisted, keeping her eye on the stick, and by stretching as far as she could, managed to catch it just before it hit the surface. And without losing her balance and falling in!

"How about that?" she demanded, wanting his verbal appreciation of her skill. "You thought I was going to. . . ." She stopped when she saw Rabbit. He was standing oddly still, looking up at the bank behind them, a silly smile frozen on his face. Turning, she saw the Major and Ed, the hunter, standing on the bank, watching them. Cold flooded through her body and she began to shiver.

"Come out of there!" The Major broke the sudden silence.

The children just looked at them, frightened into inactivity.

"Get up here!" It never occurred to a Father that one of his commands might not be instantly obeyed and the Major was instantly angry. "You, girl, you come out first!"

Tia stood where she was, waist deep in the water.

"Did you hear what I said—or do you think you will bite me, too?"

Tia said nothing. Rabbit dog-paddled a bit to keep his position, as if he thought their interrupted game would continue as soon as the men left.

The Major reached for the bow the hunter carried and began to fit an arrow into the string. Tia's move was instinctive. She dove into the water and began to swim towards the centre of the river. An arrow whizzed past her, fell harmlessly on the surface and floated away. She didn't bother to look back. If they hit her now there was nothing she could do about it, and looking back would waste valuable energy she could not afford. From the corner of her eye she saw Rabbit pull even with her and then dive. Another arrow fell ahead of her.

Suddenly there was no bottom beneath her feet and she nearly stopped swimming. She had never been in deep water before. The current became a pushing thing that carried her legs sideways and she spun down into the turbulence. She heard someone shouting from the banks. Coming up, she gasped for air, flailed her arms wildly in panic and sank down. Something hit her on the right shoulder and pushed her head back up above the surface. Rabbit shot up ahead of her. "Ff-ff-ff-float!" he finally managed to yell. "L-l-l-let it c-c-carry you!" He dived again and shoved her upwards. "B-b-back—ff-float on your b-back!"

She rolled over in the water and the ease of the roll encouraged her. But it was not easy to keep her head above the surface and she had to dog-paddle constantly to do so.

Thhhipp!

Something burned on the back of her leg and she was afraid to look. Ahead of them, on the side of the river where the Path was, she saw two more men appear. One of them dropped his pack, jumped into the water and began swimming towards Rabbit—who dived and disappeared. The swimmer turned and waited for Tia. He reached out to grab her as she floated by. There was no time to think. She struck out desperately and pushed two fingers into his right eye with all the force she could manage. The effort of her blow thrust her away from him in the water. The injured hunter yelled with pain and grabbed out blindly for her before the current rolled his body sideways and he was forced to swim towards shore to save his life.

"She *is* a witch!" she heard someone shout from the banks and then saw Rabbit's head reappear in the river ahead of her. She swam as far as she could and then floated along. The river had widened now and the men were no longer shooting at them, their poorly balanced arrows being effective only at very short range. By turning her head she could see the men running along the banks, following the two of them as they drifted with the current.

The half-open bag tied around her waist was jerking and bumping against her back as though struggling to get free. Tia twisted slightly in the water to bring it up so that she might pull it off of her. The bag popped to the surface and floated there, bouyed up by the air trapped with it. There was no way she could loosen the soaked leather cords and still keep the current from tumbling her over, so she left it and struggled on.

Ahead and to the right she saw Rabbit's back lift out of the water, and then he appeared to be standing up right on the river. Before she could think how that could be, her feet struck against sand and she was pushed sideways onto a bar. Too tired to swim any more, now that she had a chance to rest, she stumbled through the water toward her friend, breathing very hard and utterly exhausted.

Neither of them spoke as they stood together, coughing, rubbing the water out of their eyes as it dripped from their hair, the river washing around their ankles. They shared their sandbar with a collection of branches, parts of trees still sprouting leaves, and logs of various sizes washed up on the shallows. They were so near collapse that they paid little attention to the men shouting to each other across the river.

Rabbit sat down on the trunk of a tree and leaned back against its dead branches. Under his weight the tree bobbed in the water and the root end tipped up from the sandbar. The boy grabbed a branch to stabilize himself and then relaxed again as much as he could.

"Why don't they come and get us?" Tia asked, no longer caring what happened, even staring at her bleeding calf with disinterest.

"Th-they-they're afraid of you, I th-think."

"Good."

She looked up at the sky. The rain had stopped. In the water she hadn't noticed that. It was almost evening and the clouds made it darker than normal. As the pain in her chest and stomach lessened, she became more aware of the danger of their situation.

Across from them on the Path side of the river two hunters and the three soldiers waited to hear the Major's instructions. On the opposite stood Ed and the Major.

"Can you swim?" he shouted across to his men.

There was a discussion among them and then a soldier called back. "Yes . . . but we don't want to lose our eyes or die from a bite from that girl. Why don't you just leave them? Let them drown!"

"I want her taken alive!"

"Let Ed go get her!" someone bellowed.

"Are you disobeying my orders?"

"We don't see the sense in dying for a girl you're going to kill anyhow."

"Drowning is not the death I've planned for her."

"Let Ed go—he likes to be brave."

Tia turned to look at the Major. He was talking to Ed, and Ed was gesturing with his arms.

"He d-d-doesn't want to either," observed Rabbit and giggled. He rather liked having adults, and men at that, afraid of them. Even if it was Tia they feared. Then he stopped laughing. Ed was removing his leather garment. Naked except for the Missile cord around his neck, he waded into the water and began to swim toward their sandbar.

Rabbit sat up in alarm. The tree rolled dangerously in the water and then almost lifted free. Hearing his strangled shout, Tia turned to see him falling back into its branches. His weight made the tree lift its root end free of the sandbar and start to swing slowly into the main current. Without thinking she ran through the water to it and grabbed it by a root, trying to hold it back. It was no use. The current was stronger than she was and the tree pulled her along.

"G-g-get on!" yelled Rabbit. "It'll c-carry us!"

"It'll sink!" Tia was afraid. "Maybe we can make it to the bank. We can outrun the Major."

"G-get on!" Seeing her still hesitant, Rabbit

said bluntly, "If-if you try to run, th-they'll kill you for sure. Th-the tr-tree's floating—get on!"

And she did, stumbling after it through the deepening water, she pulled it sideways, nearly throwing Rabbit into the river, and by stepping on a strong projecting root, shot the branch end of the dead wood higher in the water before jumping desperately onto the rougher bark of the trunk. She slipped and came down hard astride the trunk. The pain that shot up her back was severe, and with her eyes blinded by tears she clung in a death grip to the wet roots dangling above her.

Seeing they were about to roll over, Rabbit instinctively flattened himself on the branches, trying hard to distribute his little weight as evenly as he could to compensate for Tia. The tree bobbed ominously, rolling right and then left. Each move Tia made to keep her balance rocked the roots downward into the water and lifted the branches higher. They were rocking the tree completely off the sandbar it was snagged on. As the water grew deeper, and the current swifter beneath the tree, it suddenly broke completely free and they were afloat, Rabbit lying spread-eagle in the branches, Tia astride the trunk, her back to him.

She saw Ed emerge from the water and splash

his way towards them over the sandbar, beginning to run as he realized what was happening.

"He's going to catch us! He's going to catch us!" she yelled to Rabbit, and rode the tree like a hobby-horse rider in panic, causing it to bob and jerk and roll.

"S-ssss-stop it!" Rabbit yelled back, "Ya-you're ti-tipping it again!"

And she was. But she was also rocking it farther away from the sandbar. Ed was running now in water up to his knees at the narrow end of the bar. He threw himself in with a splash and started to swim again, then, perhaps because of the swiftness of the rain-swollen current in mid-stream, he gave up and shouted, "Get back here, you little devils!"

She saw him reach back automatically for his bow before he remembered it was still on the bank with the Major. He dived, apparently hunting for something on the river bottom to throw at them. He surfaced again and called out, but Tia couldn't hear what he said.

In any event she realized they couldn't obey now even if they wanted to. Too frightened to do anything other than cling where they were, they rode their impromptu craft down the centre of the stream and drifted slowly out of sight of the angry, yelling men running along the banks after them.

I I

Everyone at Morrow had come down to the dock to see the *Simone II* and her crew off to sea on what was technically being referred to as Expedition #81. But unlike the other eighty expeditions, this one was not searching for treasures to be found in the vaults of ancient museums, or deposits of ore left unfound by the previous civilization, or even new strains of plants to be domesticated. Expedition #81 had just one purpose: to find and recover two children of Morrow.

The *Simone II,* like her sister ship, the *Elena,* which was berthed down the coast at Bonai, was designed for research and exploration. If, on occasion, they had to carry bulk cargo, deep holds in the two outer hulls were readily converted for that purpose. She was not a big ship by ancient standards; she could carry eighty people in great comfort and a hundred with a little squeezing. Nor was she fleet. Her triple hulls, while giving her an ungainly look from the rear, gave her great stability and the security needed by a ship totally alone at sea. In case of disaster, hope of rescue could come only from Morrow.

From the roof of her top deck, solar energy absorption cells to feed her powerplant sprouted like metallic butterflies. Their "wings" could be telescoped and folded flat to form a long roof fin while she traveled on stored energy.

Preparation for the long trip had been accomplished in record time; everyone had helped. Ashira had wakened the morning after the Council Meeting to see the harbor full of small boats from the outlying communities of Morrow. And all the boats had carried as many people as they could safely handle. The job of loading the big ship for the voyage, which Ashira had estimated would take three days, had taken thirty-six hours.

Now, after two days at sea with little to occupy her but her thoughts, she was tense with worry.

"I cannot understand why we haven't received anything from them," she fretted to Varas. "Their last contact was a day and a half ago. Do you suppose they have been captured? And if they were, are they still alive? Can they still have any food? I should never have told them to flee, Varas —they might have been safer in their horrible village, at least they'd have food and shelter."

"Distress is making you illogical," Varas replied calmly. "Staying in the village would have meant Tia's death. You know by this time that if anything dire had happened to either one of them, we would both be suffering splitting headaches within a flash of its happening. And my headache would be secondhand."

He took her by the arm and pulled her away from the ship's railing where sea spray was beginning to drench them. At the speed the ship was traveling it was difficult to find a spot on the deck that was dry, but he managed by opening the door of the amphibian and ushering her inside to sit with him in greater comfort.

"I don't imagine the going is any too easy for the children. For that reason they are probably very tired—in addition to being frightened. Neither of them has any control over their minds —nothing worth mentioning, at any rate. When you add up the fatigue, the fear, the lack of control—and the quite natural lack of concern of children regarding the worry of their elders—it's easy to understand their silence."

"You are trying to comfort me, Varas."

"Have I succeeded?"

"Partially," she admitted.

"I hope so—because what I've said is true. You are judging them by our standards. You can't do that. These children have already endured hardships in their normal lives that would destroy most of us. They are hardy, whatever else they may be."

They sat watching the sea through the windows of the car, lost in their own private thoughts. The water below was full of floating seaweed, great dark clumps of it that surged up with the waves and turned them almost black.

Farther north, they knew, they would come to areas of the ocean still covered by masses of green scum, stuff not quite alive but still capable of reproducing itself endlessly like an obscene virus. There had been reports of sea creatures sighted in this area on two expeditions of the distant past.

The creatures, so the old stories said, had large bulbous bodies like the ancient squid, and, like the squid, long tentacles. They were green, like the scum on which they appeared to feed. When frightened by the shadow or vibrations of the approaching ship, they had fled with great speed, diving beneath the scum and disappearing too quickly to be photographed or tracked by sonar.

Varas believed the reports to be the result of overworked imaginations, but he still hoped to see one of the creatures—preferably from a safe distance. If there were living things of that size in these waters, he thought they would more probably be some form of giant shell-less snail or slug— on the theory that the more simple the life form, the more easily it adapts.

The scum mass extended north from the top of the Baja Peninsula all the way to the Santa Barbara Channel. Because of it, that portion of the coastline had never been recharted, although it was suspected that massive earthquakes along the inland fault had long since made Morrow's charts obsolete.

As he sat there considering it all—what the world must have been like before, compared to the world he knew now—Varas sighed.

"What is it?"

"You'll laugh."

"No."

"I was wishing. . . . I was wishing I could see an elephant. Not on a viewscreen, but alive, real. Breathing. Smelling." His thoughts were wistful. "Or a great whale. Or a porpoise. They must have been wonderful things!"

"It's strange," Ashira entered into his mood,

"the old civilizations dreamed of finding extra-terrestial creatures. Yet they paid so little heed to the life forms on their own planet."

"It's a shame old Simon Morrow didn't feel the need for a pair of elephants in his Noah's ark." Varas brightened at the thought. "It would have given the end of the age of the mammals a little glamour."

"It's not over yet," Ashira reminded him. "And we still have no way of knowing what's left in the interior of the continents."

"Possibly an elephant or two?" He raised a shaggy eyebrow in amusement. "After all, if Tia's people survived. . . ."

And now Ashira did laugh at his wild hope.

I 2

Afterwards neither of them could remember much about that ride down the river. The tree had floated on, pitching up and down in the current, until both children were very sick and threw up all the water they had swallowed in their wild swim. Tia remembered only that she had kept falling asleep after she threw up and being wakened by water splashing in her face. Rabbit knew that he had been very cold and couldn't sleep and that his arms hurt from holding on so tightly.

They drifted down out of the hills through the night and into the next day. Several times the tree had nearly touched shore but they were too weak to try to jump off and swim to safety. In fact, they never even thought of doing so until later.

Tia remembered the sun had finally come out and burned down on her back, drying and warming her. The river bank on the right seemed farther and farther away, although the Path side, on the left, seemed as close as before. The woods ended and they could see no trees above them when they thought to look—only grass beyond the river bank. When their tree finally ran aground they sat where they were for a long time before thinking to move their painfully stiff arms and legs, falling off awkwardly into the water and exhaustedly crawling up onto the narrow beach of the shallow lake to faint into sleep.

It was past noon when Tia opened her eyes and groggily saw red clay sprinkled with gravel. An ant was busily exploring the area a foot from her nose, hurrying along, its feelers aquiver, pausing to inspect tiny rocks in its path before detouring around them and continuing on his errand. Upon reaching her outflung hand it stopped for a moment, then climbed up on it, making a circuitous route around the base of her thumb and then up over her knuckles and off on the other side.

She squinted in the bright light and stirred. The back of her leg hurt. She attempted to roll over and every muscle in her hurt. She rested again, then pulled herself up on her elbows and, using her right elbow as a brace, managed to twist over and sit up.

For a moment the ground spun around her. She closed her eyes and rubbed them, then slowly opened one. The ground was still turning. She closed that eye again and let her head hang still until the fuzzy feeling diminished. The next time she opened her eyes, things looked almost normal again.

A few feet from where she sat, Rabbit was lying sprawled on his back, arms akimbo, his mouth open in a snoring sleep of exhaustion. As Tia looked at him she felt her nose begining to run and sniffed a loud sniff. Rabbit did not stir. "I guess he's O.K.," she decided aloud after looking at him. But she was not sure. Her mind didn't seem to be working properly.

There was something about her leg, she remembered, and pulled it up to look at it. That one was unharmed, she noted, looking thoughtfully at the right leg before letting it slip flat again. "Let's try the other one," she said, and then, "Oh. That's what's wrong." Across the left calf was a long jagged furrow cut by one of the arrows. The cut was not deep and it did not appear to be infected, but it was puckering from drying in the hot sun and it hurt each time she moved the calf muscle.

"Better wash it off, Tia," she told herself solemnly. "Medic says keep it clean and it'll heal by itself." Medic . . . that reminded her of the Major and the other men. She wondered dimly if she and Rabbit had outrun them and decided they had. She didn't hear them around and, if they had followed, they would have probably caught up by now. She really should try to reach Ashira and tell her they were O.K., she thought. And she tried to concentrate but the effort was too much for her. It just made her headache worse. There was something else she was going to do? Oh yes! Wash the leg!

She jumped to her feet—and just about as quickly fell down with the dizzy blackspots whirling before her eyes. At the sound of her falling, Rabbit sighed deeply and turned over in his sleep. After staring stupidly at him for a moment, she stood up again, slowly this time, and drunkenly walked the few steps to the water and waded in. It made her too dizzy to lean over and splash water on the wound, so she just waded out until the water covered it, stood there for a while and then waded back to shore.

"I need food," she thought, "that's why I don't feel so good. Maybe I'd better sit down before I try to find us something to eat." She trudged up the slanting beach to where long grass fell over the small cliff at the lakeside and sat down to look around.

Away to the east she could see the river which fed the lake and beyond the lake, trees dotted the plain in increasing numbers until they became a forest. To the north on the opposite side of the lake were hills, higher hills than she had ever seen before. They had white tops that glistened in the sun. The lake stretched away to the west; she could barely see the end of it. Behind her, to the south, lay a grassy plain full of the usual tiny mounds that always covered grassy places. There were trees and bushes and flowering plants on the plain but nothing else. She could see no animals or people.

A bee zoomed past and stopped on a yellow wild rosebush nearby. Looking after it, she saw the rosebush was full of bees tumbling in and out of the flowers and finally flying off, their rear ends yellow with pollen. Bees. Busy as a bee. Honey! Bees made honey! She had helped Anna clean out a honeycomb once. Anna had given her some honey that was crystalized and delicious; the two of them had eaten all they could before carrying the rest back to the kitchen for Father Otto. But Anna had had a leather bellows and coals to set wet leaves to smoking. Even if she, Tia, could find the beehive, what was she to do about getting rid of the bees?

"I'll find the hive first," she told herself practically, "then I'll decide what to do."

By sitting still and watching, she saw that the bees all seemed to fly off in the same direction, slightly southwest. She could see their wings glinting in the sun for several hundred yards and then dipping down and disappearing. The returning bees came from the same direction. Getting slowly to her feet she headed that way.

She lost track of the bees repeatedly before finally seeing one land on a weathered gray remnant of a huge tree. The bee disappeared into a wide lightning crack in the log and as she watched, another bee emerged and seemed to raise itself up a little to feel the wind before taking off in the direction of the lake shore. When she rapped the dead wood sharply with her knuckles to hear how punky it sounded, a phalanx of bees emerged and buzzed angrily about her. She retreated as fast as she could but she had discovered what she needed to know. The log was very rotten.

She sat down on the grass to think things out.
The food bag fell between her legs and from it
wafted an odor that was decidedly foul, even to
Tia's none-too-sensitive nose. She looked down at
the bag and rather stupidly wondered why it stank
so before thinking all she needed to do to find out
was to open it. Inside were two small and very
dead fish floating in about half a cup of trapped
water.

She wrinkled her nose in disgust, emptied out
the bag and sat there letting it drip. The fish disappointed her. She had always thought fish were
so pretty. She hadn't known they smelled so when
they died. But then, she decided, most things
didn't smell too good when they were dead. She
shook the bag to let the last of the water out and
the idea suddenly occurred to her—"Why not
drown the bees?"

Filling the bag at the lake, she lugged it back
to the honey tree and poured it into the crack. For
a moment nothing moved and she thought she had
missed the hive. Then sodden bees began to creep
out, then still more. And not all were too wet to fly
and all were angry. With one mind they attacked
the enemy!

Tia ran! Each step jolted her aching head, and
the wound on her leg sent out sharp burning sensa-

tions. She ignored all sensations but one—fear. Reaching the lakeside she cleared the small cliff in one bound, the beach in two, then raced into the water and threw herself down. With the rest of her hidden, the bees aimed for her head and bare neck until she was forced to dive to get away from them. Each time she stuck her head up, a couple of them got her. By the time they gave up she was feeling very sorry she had bothered them—but not sorry enough to give up that honey.

As she dragged herself from the water she looked down the beach at Rabbit lying there. He hadn't stirred.

She would wait, she decided, as Anna had done. "Give them time to cool off," the old woman had said. Tia filled the bag with water and carried it back near the log. But the noise in the hive had subsided and, too impatient to wait, she dumped the second load into the tree and ran. By the sixth bag of water almost no bees came out of the hive.

Wrapping the sack around her neck as protection, she grabbed hold of the snag and tugged. It creaked. She tugged harder. There was a crack as the rotten wood broke away and she fell backwards onto the grass, the snag still in her hand. A handful of very wet bees fell off onto her dress and she brushed them away with the wood. Two managed to sting her on the arm. She pulled their barbs out with her teeth and returned to the log.

What she saw cheered her immensely. The snag had broken away to expose a good chunk of honeycomb. Where the comb was damaged by her violations, it dripped a thick transparent amber sweetness down the side of the gray log. Avoiding the bees crawling in it, she wiped up a handful of honey and poured it into her mouth, then another and another until the spilled stuff was gone and she realized the sun would soon dry the wet bees.

Grabbing hold of the rotten wood, she tugged small pieces away until a good portion of the hive was exposed. With a piece of punk she brushed away the bulk of the bees, unwrapped the sack from around her neck, and filled it with chunks of honeycomb. She couldn't find any of the hard honey, like the kind Anna had found. She was a little disappointed because she had wanted to bring Rabbit a special treat, but all in all she was quite pleased with herself!

Tying the sack shut and carrying it as carefully as possible to avoid breaking the comb any more than necessary, she headed back to the beach. Her face was badly stung; one eyelid drooped oddly as it ballooned outward, her arms and legs were dotted with swellings and she hurt. But she had found them food and that made up for everything else.

"Rabbit!" she called from the top of the bank, "Rabbit! Wake up! Supper is ready!"

Rabbit's mouth snapped shut like a trap and he snorted twice before shaking his head, rubbing his eyes and opening them. "Wh-where are you?"

"Up here. I've got something for us to eat!"

He rolled over quickly, started to stand up, thought better of it and crawled up the beach to her on his hands and knees.

When both of them had eaten all the honey they could hold and sat chewing the wax for its sweetness, they felt much better.

"You l-l-look f-funny!" Rabbit said, looking at Tia for the first time since waking up. "Your eyes are all p-p-puffy and your n-neck's f-f-fat!"

Tia felt her neck gingerly. "I got stung."

The little boy nodded agreement. "Ma-maybe you b-better go wash off," he suggested. "C-cold water m-makes beestings f-feel better."

They both washed the honey from themselves and off the outside of the bag since it was attracting the bees who had made it and every other insect for miles around. When they were sufficiently clean to please themselves, in other words, when their hands no longer stuck together and their skin had resumed its usual brown color, they felt their normal healthy selves again.

"Can you l-live on honey, Tia?"

"I don't know."

"M-maybe I'd better see what else we can find before we s-start off again?" he decided. "You w-worked very hard to get that honey—s-so you just rest." He started off, looking absurdly small in the open grassland.

"Don't you get lost!" Tia called after him.

"I'll stay right around here. Be-besides, you w-went off while I was ss-sleeping—and you d-didn't get lost."

"I'm older than you."

"B-but I'm just as smart! You said so!"

13

When Rabbit returned, Tia was stretched out in the shade of a tall bush-like tree, her arms, neck and most of her face covered with wet mud.

"Wha-what ha-happened? You l-look ta-ter-rible!"

"Ashira said it would make it feel better."

"Oh? When?"

"While you were gone." Tia got up to see what Rabbit had brought as he dumped a pile of stuff from his shirt. "They said we were by a lake that's on their map and that we'd come a long way—and there used to be a dam here, a big one, and we should follow the water west and it would bring us to The Sea—like they said before. They seemed very excited to know where we were—I told her about how high the hills were and everything."

"D-did she ss-say when they'd find us?"

"No," admitted Tia.

Rabbit thought about it for a moment, then shrugged. What couldn't be helped wasn't worth worrying about. "L-look what I found!"

What he found were puffballs in a variety of sizes and states of edibility, along with almost a quart of round reddish berries. They ate the berries quickly and found them very good. The puffballs tasted strange but they quickly found that if they dipped them in honey, the sweetness covered almost all the taste of the mushrooms. And the bulk seemed to fill their stomachs.

"I wish we had some meat," Tia said as she chewed a puffball.

"I w-wish we had fire."

"And some blankets."

"And s-s-some pa-potatoes to roast in the f-fire—"

"Then we wouldn't have to worry about anything . . ." Tia stopped, remembering the Major and the hunters, "well, at least we wouldn't have to worry about some things."

"At least I d-don't have to be in s-s-school," Rabbit was obviously trying to look on the bright side, "and you don't have to work in the ff-fields

—or wash dishes and c-carry out slop from the kitchen and th-things like that."

Tia thought back over the life she had left behind. And for all the fear and hardship of their journey, she knew she preferred the trip to her old life at the Base. She had never tasted freedom in any form and she found it very satisfying.

"We'd better start walking," she said abruptly. "We've got a long way to go to meet the ship."

"C-can't we stay here awhile? It's n-nice here."

"We'll walk along the lake—it'll still be nice."

Packing the remaining mushrooms into the honey bag, they started off. It was easy walking along the lake shore for the most part, and when it got boggy or too full of reeds along the beach, they detoured to hard ground. They stopped to rest and eat at sunset and then continued walking until long after dark. The wind off the lake was cold that night, and they slept only fitfully, huddled together in the protection of some low bushes.

By afternoon of the next day the shores of the lake had grown higher and steeper until there was no beach left to follow, and they climbed up to follow the cliff above the water. The hill was covered with pine and scrub grass over hard clay. Here and there were more berry bushes in the sunny openings between the pine trees, and the two of them stopped often to pick and eat the ripe berries.

The low hills curved around the lake shore and they followed the curve to find the river Ashira said must lead from the lake. On a particularly high spot they stopped and climbed up to the top of a rock and looked back to see if they were being followed. There was no sign of any other living creature. The winds blew across an empty brownish plain, dotted with trees and an occasional rock pile.

"I b-b-bet nobody's ever been here before!" Rabbit said suddenly, "Not the Fathers or hunters or anybody! No people in all the time this has been here!" And as he looked at Tia a big smile spread over his face and it seemed to her that he no longer looked so much like his namesake. Some of the . . . she didn't know the right word . . . 'sneakiness' was gone. Sensing her thought, he said, "You d-don't look so scared either, like you always d-did."

"I never looked scared!"

"Oh yes!" he said, "You always l-looked scared back home—like you thought someone was g-going to h-hit you all the time—and they did p-pretty often—and you always went around with your eyes half ss-shut—like you didn't want p-people to see in and you d-didn't want to see them much either."

"I don't like our people very much," Tia admitted. "Not most of them anyway. They were mean to us, Rabbit—I mean, everybody was mean to everybody, but . . ."

"B-b-b-but they were m-m-meaner to us!" concluded Rabbit and nodded agreement.

He sat down abruptly on the sunwarmed stone, picked a strand of grass growing from a crevice and began to suck on it thoughtfully. Tia sat down beside him. The honeybag squelched as she placed it between her legs to keep it from tipping over.

"You kn-know what?"

"What?"

"I'm ga-glad we had to run away!"

"Me too," said Tia fervently.

"Let's not ever go back!—even when we're all grown up!"

"No," said Tia, who was old enough to know they had no choice in the matter, "we won't. Want some honey?" She opened the bag and dug out a section of dripping honey cone.

"Tia?"

"Uhm?"

"What will we do with the lady from the dream and those other people?"

"Live with them, I guess—that's what she said

once—that we should be living with them and belong there."

"S-she sss-eems ni-nice. Do you—" he paused, half embarrassed, "do you th-think she'd be ss-sorta like a—a m-mother?"

"No," decided Tia, after some thought of what she knew of mothers at the Base, "I think she'll be much nicer than that."

An hour's walk brought them within sound of the falls flowing over the remains of the once great dam now broken by earthquakes and the pressure of silt in the lake behind it. As they stood on the hill overlooking the dam, the children did not recognize it. The largest dam they knew was the one forming the frog pond in the creek running through the settlement. To them, this old spillway was simply a waterfall. From the hill they could see the falls entered a pool below, feeding into an area of marsh before the river reformed. They picked their way down the slope and around the marsh.

Orange and brown butterflies danced in the late afternoon sunshine and scattered in colourful clouds as the children hurried along, sloshing through small streams and climbing spongy hummocks of earth until they reached the river proper again. The river was narrow here and deeper than it had been before entering the lake; it seemed to cut its way through the ground. The banks were crumbly, and the children could see where huge chunks of soil and grass had broken off and tumbled into the water. They walked well away from the edge.

By nightfall they were following a path along the river as smooth and green as the path through the woods had been. On both sides of the river the ground was covered with mounds, some of them very large. Climbing to the top of one that was higher than usual, Rabbit made a discovery.

"L-look at the shadows!" he called to Tia.

Half scared by his excitement, Tia looked around her. She didn't see anything unusual from there on the path.

"No-no—come up here with me," he said and when she joined him, he pointed south and then north across the river. "L-look at the sh-shadows!" he repeated, "they make straight lines!"

The mounds lay in almost perfect rows, outlined by shadows in the rills between them. Only the occasional trees growing up out of the depressions broke the gridlike pattern of shadow and sunlit golden grass.

"That's pretty!" Tia said.

"B-but why do they do that?" Rabbit wanted to know.

"I suppose people did it," Tia said, but she didn't sound sure of herself. "What did they say about it in school?"

"We n-n-never talked about mounds."

He continued to look at the phenomenon. "Why would p-people do something like this? Did they plant things here?"

"No," Tia said slowly, as though remembering something she had dreamed and forgotten long ago, "They lived here I think. I think the mounds cover the places where their houses were a long time ago. When the houses fell down, dust and ground blew over them and grass began to grow. Ashira said we should come to a thing called a City where a lot of people used to live. . . ."

"They built their houses on mm-mounds?"

"I don't know—but the mounds have something to do with people, I think."

"Well," said Rabbit, "if it was p-people, they cer-certainly made pretty places!"

The mounds grew higher the further they walked. The river turned towards the southwest and they traveled between small hills on both sides of the water. Some of the hills had rocky caves in them that seemed like black squares of total darkness.

"Let's ss-stop," Rabbit said, after a while, "I

d-don't want to walk p-past everything in the dark. Let's get a drink and th-then go f-find a cave we can ss-sleep in tonight."

The cave they chose was in an outcropping of pebbly white rocks near the path. They chose it because it was the one they could most easily see. Only the roof and one wall remained intact; the floor was covered with sand and what appeared in the darkness to be weeds. The sand was still warm from the heat of the sun and they stretched out in comfort, glad to be out of the wind and warm for the night.

14

Mist was still rising from the river when they awoke in the morning and resumed their journey along its bank. With their view blocked by mounds of grass-covered rubble on their left, the children had no idea of the size of the place they had entered until the river swung out around a promontory and looped again to the west. They stopped at the curve of the river and stood and stared at what they saw, their mouths hanging open in wonder, their empty stomachs forgotten.

Nothing they had ever heard of, or thought, or imagined had prepared them for this. The Major had spoken of a long lost Paradise where men had built houses taller than trees. But no one could really believe it. It was just a myth handed down from Father to Father. And yet here stood the skeletons of what were obviously the remains of these houses.

"B-b-boy!" exploded Rabbit, "l-l-look at that!"

Deserted for more years than either of them could imagine, the city lay in the sunlight that exposed its devastation. Hills of cement rubble no grass could cover marked the collapse of many structures. Two stone walls and part of the bell tower of what had once been an immense cathedral stood on a hill to the south. In the center of the desolation the structural core of almost a dozen tall buildings still stood, some of them leaning dangerously, high skeletal towers reaching up into nothingness.

A wasp buzzed past them, her body weighted by the mud she carried from the riverbank, and flew towards the remains of an old building. The sound of the insect broke the children from their spell. Without another word they began to run along the path, searching for an opening in the piles of rubble which would lead them toward the towers.

But an opening was not easy to find here, for when the buildings fell they had thrown small mountains of bricks, enormous slabs of concrete and twisted piles of rusting steel across what were once streets. Rubble strewn across the path sometimes forced the children to edge along the water and several times they had to climb over the dangerously sliding talus of ruin. After two of these trips over talus, Tia's initial enthusiasm began to ebb.

"Maybe we should just look at them from here?" she suggested. "What if we fall in something—or get hurt?"

"B-b-but we mm-might never see anything like this again," Rabbit reminded her.

"That's O.K.," said Tia, "it's all broken and sad anyhow."

"Please, Tia? Can't we j-just ll-look a l-little?"

"Well—O.K.—but let's head down that way," she said, pointing further along the path, "That looks like an open space. Maybe it leads somewhere."

Rabbit needed no further urging. He ran ahead to explore the possibility. "It's a n-new path," he shouted to her. "Open!"

The ancient boulevard through the center of the business district had been built wide to show off the buildings bordering it. Even when those buildings had collapsed, the boulevard was still so wide that the debris couldn't completely cover it. Rain

washing down from the rubble had made a dry
creek bed between the mounds, and Tia and Rabbit followed its twisting course into the ruins.

Like tourists in a strange city, they stopped
often, shaded their eyes with their hands and
looked up to see the tops of the structures. Pillars
that once housed elevators stood in geometric pre-
cision towering above everything; steps of cement
and eroded metal zig-zagged up to end in mid-air.
In the center of their path they came upon an ancient aluminum eagle that had once been mounted
hundreds of feet above the street. It lay now on its
back in the dust, grayed and pitted with age.

The children stopped to look at it. Tia reached
out tentatively and ran her brown hand over the
still-smooth curve of its cruel beak.

"What do you suppose that was?"

"I th-think it was a b-bird . . . that's what
they called things that flew in the air like b-bugs
but th-they didn't look like bugs. That's what
F-father Neal said."

"Was this one ever alive?"

"I d-don't know—but I d-don't think so. I think
they m-made it."

Tia looked at it a long time—the fierce beak, the
sharp claws that seemed to be wrapped around
something unrecognizable. "It's not very pretty,"

she decided finally. "Maybe real birds were better."

Ahead of them now they could see the remains of a tall building standing like a barrier across the valley formed by the hills of ruin. A massive oblong pile of stone, it was almost completely covered by the collapse of its tower and the surrounding buildings. Only the front of it had accidentally escaped entombment.

Half an hour's walk brought the children to its base. They found a small area directly in front of the building free of fallen stones and covered with tall grass and shrubs grown to almost tree size. In a stone pool rainwater stood, green and stagnant. In one spot a rose bush sprawled over the ground and partially covered the sandy steps to the entrance. At the top of the steps huge doors of badly corroded metal hung open, frozen there by the weight of the building settling in decay.

"C-come on!" Rabbit called excitedly, running up the steps. "This l-looks like a good one!" But in the yard-wide opening between the buckling double doors he stopped and waited for her to catch up.

They walked together into the dimness of the great lobby and stood looking up. Directly opposite the entrance, broad stone steps led to a balcony that encircled the lobby. On both sides of the steps were empty shafts and, flanking them, dark tunnels too black to see into. Dusty beams of light flooded into the huge room from the window openings directly beneath the ceiling. Sections of the ceiling had fallen to the floor below and more hung precariously creaking in a wind the children could not feel. Icicles of stalactites dripped from seeping seams. The walls were stained with the rains of centuries.

Wordlessly the two of them headed up the staircase to the balcony, the stillness magnifying the soft plat-plat of bare feet in the dust. Beyond the staircase another lobby opened into walls lined with metal doors. Through the few of them that hung open the children could see down into deep pits, and hear the wind moan in the darkness.

Tia stood at the top of the stairs and looked down at the hall below them and the ceiling still high overhead. "I wonder what they used it for?" she whispered, intimidated by the vastness and the old silence.

"Mm-maybe it was a b-barn of some kind?" suggested Rabbit, and the walls echoed "kind-kind-kind" in the dimness.

Tia shivered and goosebumps dotted her bare arms. "Come on," she said, "let's look around and then get out of here."

"I w-want to climb to the top and look out."

They explored the balcony where lack of rubble permitted passage. There wasn't much left to see. Cave-like openings off its surface were dark and full of debris. The dim hall behind the balcony was much more promising—at least it was open. At its end another hall ran parallel to the vast lobby below and opening off this were more doorways. And there were the deep pits. To the right, the hall had collapsed. They turned left and headed towards a window opening, taking care to step only where the floor was bare and sandy beneath their feet lest they cut themselves on sharp stones.

The hallway made a sharp turn and there were stone stairs, still passable, leading both up and down. Rabbit automatically started up and Tia followed. The doors on the floor landings had fallen in, but the individual floors were impassable. After ten short flights they could see the sky above them. The steps became covered with decomposing bricks. Picking their way over the debris they emerged on what had once been the roof of the first tier of the huge building and they stood and looked out on the scene below.

Behind them was a small mountain formed by the rest of the building. Before them was the path they had followed all the way to the river that gleamed blue in the morning light. The river was flanked on both sides, as far as they could see, by the remains of the city. Far off to the east was the shine of the lake and behind it, the mountains.

"This must have been a good place to live," Tia said finally, "before it all fell down."

Rabbit nodded absentmindedly, too busy looking to talk now. He walked away from Tia, towards the low brick wall rimming the ancient terrace. There was a sharp crack and part of the railing broke off and fell to the ground below. Rabbit jumped back to the comparative safety of the stairs. The vibrations from the movement of even his small weight sent another section of the railing tumbling. They listened to the bricks cracking against each other as they fell. The children stood still for a long time, afraid to move for fear the stairs would collapse, too. When minutes passed and nothing further happened, they took deep breaths of relief and began to enjoy the view again.

Hills blocked the west and south, where the highest buildings seemed to have stood. The grid-like outline of city blocks that Rabbit had noted the evening before was no longer apparent from up here where the sunlight removed all shadow. He was looking east, trying to figure out where they had spent the night, when he saw something that made him cry out in surprise.

"L-l-look!" He pointed.

Following the direction indicated by his grubby hand, Tia looked. For a moment she saw nothing. Her eyes began to water from the sun and she closed them hard to clear the tears. When she looked again she thought she saw something move, far away almost at the lake. She squinted for a better view and then realized what they were looking at was a small cloud of dust or smoke.

"It's them!" It was a wail of disappointment and fear. Try as hard as they could, they could see no one moving. The cloud seemed to stay in one place.

"I th-think th-they're smoking meat," Rabbit finally whispered—as if afraid his enemies would overhear him. "They wouldn't make that much smoke just to cook."

"That means they're going to follow us for a long time!" Tia suddenly felt very tired. She had hoped they had lost the men, that they would give up when they escaped from them on the river. Finding this was not the case depressed her. "We'd better go, she said as she shook off the panic.

It was harder going down the steps than coming up. The rubble on the stairs could be stepped over going up. Going down, with no railing, picking their way over crumbling cement and stones, was a nerve-wracking business.

Both of them were sweating by the time they reached the hall below and headed for the staircase to the lobby. The building that had seemed such a mystery less than an hour ago now seemed like a trap and they wanted nothing more than to get out of it.

There was no stopping now to marvel over the size of the place, or even the fact that it was still more or less standing. The slap of their bare footsteps in the dust echoed through the deserted halls as they ran. The old walls sent back the rasp of their ragged breathing. They fled down the wide stairs and dodged around the piles of rubble on the lobby floor.

They were halfway across the lobby when a quaking noise overhead made Tia glance up. To her horror she saw one of the ceiling sections above them tearing loose, dangling from a set of rusty rods. With a yelp of fright she grabbed for Rabbit and rolled with him sideways under an overhang of debris on the floor.

"Wha. . . ?" was all the startled boy had time to ask before the plasticized stone panel broke free and came crashing down where they had been only a moment ago.

The lobby walls reverberated with the crash.

Chunks and chips and dust of stone flew, stinging at them, covering their skin, filling their hair and eyes. Shock waves of sound shook smaller, individual pieces into dropping from ceiling and walls. Then, as suddenly as it began, it was over. Silence returned slowly, occasionally broken by the rattle of fragments of the broken panel rolling from the pile to the floor.

For minutes afterwards Tia and Rabbit huddled under their shelter, afraid to move and shaking for fear that if they did not move, the entire building might come down on top of them. A blue mud wasp, searching for the nest she had built on the now-destroyed panel zzzzzed her anger somewhere above them.

"Are you O.K.?" Tia finally whispered to Rabbit, brushing some fragments out of his tangled hair.

"I th-th-think so," he managed to answer. "I-I'm not su-sure I c-c-can stand up. My knees are sh-shaking so m-much!" He reached over and brushed dirt from her face, shyly, as though to reassure himself of her presence. "Are you O.K.?"

She nodded, not trusting herself to speak, then caught his hand and squeezed it. "Come on," she whispered, "let's crawl out and look—but be careful!"

If they hadn't heard the crash, they would have had no way of knowing the panel had fallen. To the casual eye the lobby floor looked no different than it had when they entered. Cautiously they stood erect and looked up at the ceiling. After assuring themselves there was no further immediate danger from above, they tiptoed the rest of the way across the lobby and out into the welcome sunshine of the little park.

I5

By nightfall they had covered many miles. Hills of ruin still kept them edging along the river, but now the hills were lower and many were covered with vegetation. The children had passed areas so desolate not even the sound of an insect was heard, where the ground was bare of all life and the river seemed to flow over a bed of dark red earth. Here long cement foundations supporting nothing stuck out into the river; behind them on the shore enormous mounds of red slag towered as high as the biggest ruins. The wind had blown earth from the mounds into drifts rilled by erosion. Where the wind swept the earth clean, it exposed curious parallel tracks running toward the cement structure in the river.

The children passed huge round skeletons of corroded metal, so many that they seemed like some bizarre fungus growth. Where these stood the riverbed was black muck and the water covered with a thin film of irridescent slime.

Tia and Rabbit spoke little as they walked; they had no words for what they were seeing. It was just there, like the abundance of sacred relics they stepped over, relics far more perfect than those housed in the vault of the church at the Base. Relics of glass turned amethyst by the sun burning through the oxygen-depleted air, warped and slowly rotting plastic containers, tiles and bricks, bits of metal still not absorbed by the earth, all were there for the taking.

They rested twice during their march, ate some of the honey rapidly leaking from the bag in the heat, and drank from the river where the water seemed fit for consumption. Hunger was an ever-present thing now, and they began to feel light-headed and weak. Yet they were afraid to stop.

"If they're smoking meat, they'll stay there at least two days," Tia reasoned. "It takes that long to dry it out enough to carry."

"If they stop to pick up relics for the Major, it'll take longer," came Rabbit's thought.

They kept on walking, staggering slightly. The moon rose and was high overhead before they fell in exhaustion and slept where they fell, Tia's hand reaching out to touch Rabbit's arm.

If they dreamed that night neither remembered

it. They woke before dawn and were aware of a strange smell in the wind. As they sat eating the last of the honey Rabbit began sniffing.

"The s-smell is coming from the water," he announced.

Tia got up stiffly and walked closer to the river. He was right. It was still too dark to see much more than the shimmer of the river but it seemed to her it was higher than it had been the night before.

"Maybe there was a storm somewhere and new water is coming downstream?"

"W-we didn't get wet."

Tia accepted this in silence. She had already lost interest in the river; her mind was on food. She knew they must find some soon or they would die. Her inborn weakness had always shamed her, and now the refusal of her body to heed her commands about something as simple as walking a straight line alarmed her to the point where it almost replaced the fear of the men following them.

"Come on," she said, coming back to where he sat still scraping the last of the honey from the sodden sides of the leather bag. "We might as well start walking before it gets hot. When the sun comes up, we can look for something to eat."

Rabbit sighed but struggled to his sore feet and

followed after her, the bag hanging limply from his sticky hand.

The river grew pink with morning light and the children saw that it was much higher than it had been the night before. It was also considerably wider. Out in the center of the channel stood a series of massive stone platforms that stretched out from shore to shore and continued on up the banks. Beyond the stone platform by the river's edge the rubble mounds abruptly ended and were replaced by a small wood.

A path marked by white stone blocks and used now only by rabbits snaked across the forest floor. It was entirely covered by leaves and pine needles in some places but still plainly visible as it wound up a small hill or curved around the gnarled base of an ancient tree.

Leaving the riverbank temporarily to explore the wood for food, they found little but yellow mushrooms growing like shelves from fallen trees. These were all too tough to chew. The path stretched invitingly up over a small hill and they followed and were surprised to see the gleam of the river far ahead of them where no river should have been.

"Let's go this way," Tia decided, "It's cooler here under the trees."

"D-do-do you th-think s-s-someone lives around here?" The thought had obviously just occurred to Rabbit and had just as obviously scared him.

"Why?" Tia's heart beat faster at the idea.

"Be-because I hear a f-f-funny noise. Listen!"

Tia listened. There was the sound of the wind moving leaves above them, a few insect noises—and then she heard it, too—a faint sloshing noise as if someone were pouring out buckets of dishwater. But in a volume that was beyond her imagination. As she listened the sound came again and then again and again until its very constancy gave her confidence. No person was strong enough to do anything that often in that volume.

"D-do you hear it?"

"It's not people."

Rabbit let out a big sigh of relief, "B-but what do-do you think it is?"

"Let's go see."

They ran along the path, kicking pine cones out of their way, jumping over branches and, when they reached a slight grade, stumbling several times. At the top of the hill they saw the water beyond and the whitecapped surf moving toward shore in orderly rows. Tia stopped short.

"There's no bank on the other side!" she whispered in awe.

Catching her thoughts Rabbit shouted, "SSSS-SSSEA! It's the SS-SEA!"

And they began to run like wild things toward the water, stumbling through the deep sand, jumping over lines of tidal wrack, oblivious to everything else but the beckoning gleam and rush of the ocean, they went down across the wet sand and into the foam of an incoming wave.

The water sloshed around them with a force foreign to them. Rabbit very quickly discovered he could hardly keep his balance against the waves and staggered back towards the shore. Tia, enraptured by it all, stood with the water up to her hips and felt the waves surge around, making her body buoyant, trying to lift her. She felt the tickle of small shells and gravel flowing across her feet, the push of the current as the waves came in and receded.

"Hey," called Rabbit, "Wh-wh-where are the dream p-people? Isn't this The Ss-s-sea they were s-showing us?"

"Maybe they haven't come yet—Ashira said it was a long way. How many days have we been walking?"

Rabbit shrugged. He couldn't remember.

"They're coming from the south—maybe we should walk that way and meet them?"

There were snail shells everywhere along the beach, some of them almost a foot across. They lay free on the sand, or half-buried, or stuck to the dried tangles of tidewashed kelp. In the shallows and the protected areas behind sandbars were dozens of the living creatures. They flowed across the sandy bottom, their frilly, fleshy deep-orange mantles almost concealing their striated brown shells, tiny eyes gleaming brightly on eyestalks. The surging current from a high wave would flow around them, causing their mantles to wave like laver in the tidal ebb, and they would pause in their forward flow and flatten themselves closer to the sandy floor until the current subsided.

The children watched in horrified fascination as one orange mantled monster approached three smaller snails. Without hesitation it proceeded on its way as though the others did not exist, flowing up and over them. The mantles of the smaller snails disappeared beneath their shells and small jets of sand spouted upwards in the water. The large snail halted on the middle snail and flattened itself to fit the curvature of the smaller shell. The two shells rocked gently in the pool, locked together in an embrace. The other two small snails suddenly revived, extended their mantles and moved away from the joined pair.

"They look like they're running," Rabbit mentally observed.

Tia nodded, never taking her eyes off the big snail. For some minutes the children stood watching until Rabbit grew bored and wanted to move on.

"No," said Tia, "I want to see what they're doing."

"Let's pick them up." Rabbit stepped into the pool.

"Don't touch them!" Tia grabbed his arm and pulled him back. "You don't know—they might bite!"

As if disturbed by Rabbit's shadow that now hung over it, the big snail disengaged itself from the other shell and slipped off through the shallows. The top of the shell it left behind appeared a bit muddy, small bubbles escaped from it to break on the surface. A wave broke over the beach and sloshed into the pool. When the water cleared again, the shell suddenly rose and floated to the surface.

Before Tia could stop him, Rabbit grabbed for it and pulled it out onto the sand. There was a large, neatly drilled round hole on the top of the shell. The sun shining down into the hole illuminated the perfectly geometric curve of the structure created by the animal. As Rabbit tipped the shell a thin trickle of matter spilled out from a hidden curve. The shell was empty.

"The b-b-b-big one ate it!"

Tia swallowed rapidly. "Let's keep away from them," was all she said.

"Well—I g-g-guess he got hungry," said Rabbit. "I'm hungry, t-too. Let's find something to eat."

They walked along the edge of The Sea, the waves washing away their footprints in the wet sand, then made their way across the beach to some trees to rest in the shade. A hollow in the ground behind them indicated that once a building with a very deep cellar had stood there. Growing out of the center of the hollow was a tree of medium height. Rabbit lay staring at it for a long time before it occurred to him that some of what he thought were leaves must be fruit. He scrambled to his feet and hurried over to it.

"What is it?" Tia was only mildly interested in fruit.

Rabbit plucked one of the green fruits and squeezed it. It felt soft as if it were ripe. He bit into it. The outside was tough and hard to bite. He pulled some of the skin away with his teeth and looked at the pulp beneath. It was golden green and it tasted good. He squashed some against his

teeth with his tongue and it mashed nicely.
Quickly he yanked the rest of the skin off and ate
the pulp around the large seed. Excited by his
find, he picked as many of the oval-shaped fruits
as he could carry. Coming back to Tia he tossed
two of them into her lap.

"But they're green—we'll get sick."

"No-no—they're soft inside. They're ripe—try
one."

Tia ate three before she had enough. When she
had finished she felt much better. Although she
was still not completely satisfied, her stomach was
full. Rabbit, who had gone exploring in the area
while she sat and ate, returned to announce the discovery of water. "N-n-not very good water—but it
tastes b-better than your old Ss-sea." It was from a
brackish spring welling up among the trees.

"Where should we go now?" Rabbit asked when
they had drunk all they could hold. "We can't
wait here."

"That way, south—and hope we find Ashira before the Major finds us."

"We b-better t-tell her where we're at."

"I tried a little while ago but I must be too
tired. But she's smart—she'll find us. They'll be
here soon."

"I hope so," said Rabbit, "I'm s-s-still hungry."

16

They followed the coast south. After the first few days passed and no one appeared to be following them, they gradually relaxed and stopped looking back.

They lived on wild fruit and shellfish, Rabbit having decided that if snails could eat other snails, so could they. But the orange snails did not taste very good; the big clams proved too tough to chew once they had battered them open on rocks, and the oysters were too small for the work involved in opening them. That left the mussels; plentiful, thin-shelled and delicious. Having discovered by experiment that the smaller ones were the most tender, the children ate these in great quantity.

The wood near the ruined city had long since given way to high sand dunes and beyond these, grasslands and scrub pine. Drinking water came from brackish streams flowing down to meet the sea. They slept in the hollows of dunes, burying themselves in the sand to keep warm at night.

The easy walking, plenty of protein, abundant oxygen at sea level—and the genuine fun of playing in the waves whenever they felt like it, all served to produce a euphoria in the two children. After all, they told each other, they had taken care of themselves for a long time now, almost two weeks maybe, and the "Dream people" would soon find them. And with that goal in mind, they kept walking, from sunrise to sunset, taking time out only to eat and rest.

Late one afternoon they stopped to gather mussels clinging to a rock outcropping spattered with tidepools. Rabbit, who was extraordinarily hungry, stood knee-deep in water, tugging the shells away from their sessile bindings, smashing them against the rock and eating them where he stood.

Tia had filled her skirt full of shells and retreated to eat on a fairly dry spot out of the reach of the breakers. She liked to open all the mussels at once, lay them in a neat sun-burst and admire the midnight blue of the shell's rim fading into the pearly nacre cupping the animal inside. Once the shellfish were ready, she pulled an avocado from the food sack, peeled it with her teeth and placed it in the center of the shells on the clean rock. Reaching into the sack again she retrieved an over-ripe lime foraged the day before. Kneading it severely, she reduced the insides to pulp, broke it open and squeezed the juice over the avocado and mussels. The living shellfish squirmed with discomfort at this treatment.

Rabbit, watching her preparations from where he stood, called, "By-by the t-time you get ready to eat, I'm almost ff-finished."

"I get tired of them tasting the same all the time," she explained, "the fruit juice seems to help."

"You wouldn't get me to eat that," thought Rabbit, who was a purist. Even at the Base he had eaten only one thing at a time from his plate, generally starting with the vegetable, which he liked least and working his way down to his favourite, usually the meat.

Tia set to work on her first mussel, raking it out with a practiced forefinger and sliding it into her mouth. She alternated each mussel with a bite of avocado. As she ate she watched the sun sinking lower on the horizon, turning The Sea a deep blue and illuminating the shallows with silver. It was the time of day she liked best and she was enjoying it and her meal with equal pleasure when she heard Rabbit give a short grunt of disgust.

"Yuggh!"

She looked out to see what he had found and saw him kicking with his right leg, as if trying to dislodge something heavy. On the third kick he managed to bring his leg up out of the water and she saw the vivid orange mantle of one of the big snails slide from the foot and hit the water with a splash. As Rabbit half slipped from his perch on the algae-coated rock, she jumped up from her dinner and ran to him. He recovered his balance. Bracing himself with one hand against the rock, he lifted the right foot from the water again and looked at it, made a face and turned to make his way to shore. He met her halfway and splashed past without looking up.

"What is it, Rabbit? Did you hurt yourself?"

He didn't answer but continued on up the rock outcropping and sat himself down gingerly near her dining spot. Tia hurried after him.

"What happened?"

He still didn't answer but lifted up his foot instead for her to see. Blood was welling from the top of the foot and starting to drip onto the rock.

With a sick feeling she knelt beside him and

looked at the foot, then carefully splashed water over it so she could see the wound.

"I d-d-didn't even f-f-feel it until it bit!" There was quiet astonishment in his voice. "Th-there was this real b-bad sting—I l-looked down—and there it was, all oozing over my ff-foot."

The snail's sharp radula had removed a good two-inch circle of skin from the top of the foot. As Rabbit had no fat to spare, the wound left the muscle sheath exposed and gleaming with blue-white iridescence in the slanting sunlight before blood covered it again. Tia had no idea how bad the wound was, just that any wound now was serious and this one looked as if it would be very sore.

"We'll let it bleed a little," she announced with feigned calmness. "Anna said it was good to let things bleed—it cleans them out if there is any stuff in them—then we'll wash it off good." She looked around wistfully, "I wish we had something to tie it up with." But there was nothing.

When she felt it had bled enough she washed the wound repeatedly with sea water and had Rabbit hold his fingers above it until the bleeding stopped. She covered it gently with leaves of wine red laver, they being the closest thing to cloth she could find, and tied the laver on with ribbons of kelp. Rabbit sat very still while she tended to him. He never winced and said it did not hurt unless he moved the foot—but then it burned.

Done with doctoring, Tia tried to finish her food but she was no longer hungry. She ate three more mussels just because she thought she should and threw the remains of the fruit into the sea.

She heard a clicking sound and saw that Rabbit's teeth were chattering. "We'd better get out of the wind. It's nearly dark."

Rabbit nodded jerkily, his teeth not allowing him to speak.

"Can you walk?"

"Sh-sh-sure."

He stood up easily and then winced as his foot received his full weight. He would have toppled over if Tia had not caught him. "Put your arm around my neck and hang on." She put her arm around him and half carried him across the jutting rocks to the beach, then looked around, searching for a spot out of the wind.

"Hold on to me and see if you can hop up there." She pointed to two huge boulders lying halfway up the beach. Slowly, painfully, they made their way up there. Rabbit waited while she dug a hollow, helped him first sit and finally lie down in it. Putting the food bag under the injured foot as a cushion, she covered the rest of him up with sand.

He was asleep before she finished.

Rabbit dreamed of the ship that night; it appeared as a phantom thing moving over the ocean in the dark, its solar sails pale under the moon. Green and gold lights glowed from its sides, and now and then a broad white beam would sweep out over the water again and again as though signaling. In the dream, Varas was calling to him and he tried to answer.

Tia was wakened by Rabbit talking in his sleep and, reaching out, she touched his forehead and smoothed back his shaggy black hair. His skin felt warmer than usual. She touched her own face; it felt cool in the night air.

17

"We've found human footprints!" Mark reported to Ashira, "But more than just two people—looks like at least six. Whoever they were, they built a campfire."

The *Simone II* lay at anchor a few miles off the river mouth. She could go no closer to shore because silt from the river had filled the old harbor. While Ashira and Varas attempted to reach the children by telepathic area scan, Mark had taken a landing party ashore in the amphibian in the hope of finding them. Since they were not on the beach, he was following the river upstream.

"Are they children's footprints?"

"It's hard to tell—they've drifted with sand— but they all look relatively small."

"Which way are they walking?"

"Out—toward the beach. We'll turn around and track them."

"That means the children were still being pursued," Varas remarked more to himself than Ashira. It was clear that if the children had been captives, the party would not have camped and continued on toward the Sea.

"And it explains why Tia and Rabbit didn't wait here for us. But it doesn't explain why they haven't contacted us." Ashira was very worried. Although it might have been unrealistic, she had somehow expected to see the children patiently waiting for them when the *Simone II* anchored offshore.

"They are used to contacting us at one definite place," Varas was trying to comfort her fears, "perhaps our movement has left them at a loss."

"There is the chance they accidentally drowned." Lora's imagery did nothing for Ashira's peace of mind. "You said they were living on honey—they might have been very weak by the time they got this far. . . ."

"More tracks!" Mark's jubilant report cut in. "We're about five miles south of the river mouth. Looks like the children cut across the sand to pick some fruit—one set of prints is very small. Yes! Takai just found a half-eaten avocado! She's following them on foot now—we're behind her in the car. The tracks are leading back to the edge of the water. I can see the footprints of a separate group—they were following the others—the same prints we saw back at the campsite."

The car cruised along after the footprints until both sets disappeared, erased by the tide, then reappeared, only to be erased again.

"So wherever they are now, they're to the south of us."

"Come back to the ship, Mark," Ashira ordered. "We have no time to lose."

"Wouldn't it be better if we followed the beach in the amphibian?" Mark suggested. "Jemmel could follow us with the ship. We don't stand a chance of spotting them from the ship. We can't come in close enough to shore because of the rocks. And if Tia isn't in contact, we'll have to find them by sight."

"Without the generating unit on the amphibian you've only got about three hours power in the batteries," Ashira reminded him. "Then you'll have to come back aboard to recharge. How rotten was the fruit Takai found they'd eaten from?"

"Very!" replied Takai.

"Then they are at least two or three days away by now. Come back to the ship, they're beyond

your power range. If they are still free, their
trackers will build another fire tonight. We'll look
for that."

When the landing party was aboard, the *Simone
II* raised anchor and sailed rapidly south, keeping
as close to shore as she could. Lookouts equipped
with high-powered telescopes scanned the shore-
line.

Midnight came and nothing had been seen.

"I am going to bed." Varas was standing at the
upper deck railing with Ashira. "If there is anyone on that beach, they've long since gone to sleep
and their fire is nothing but embers. Either that or
they built it behind the rocks. I am nothing but a
mass of cold and dampness."

"I'll come in soon," Ashira promised to his unspoken suggestion as she kissed him on the cheek.
"Good night."

For minutes after he curled up in his bed, Varas
was too cold to sleep. Then, slowly, the electric
blanket took the deep chill from him and he
drifted off, his mind mulling over the frustrations
of the day.

At first he thought the dream was his, that he
was dreaming of the ship. But the ship looked
wrong—and his body felt so small. Something
hurt. Something was burning—a foot?—a small

brown foot—but not his foot. A boy—a small boy —Rabbit? Rabbit!

No answer. Varas received an image of a snail, slippery-orange—disgusted fear.

Rabbit? Is that you? Rabbit?

He projected the image to Ashira just as Rabbit's fevered mind called out "Tia—help me, Tia. It burns, it burns so much—our ship's out there, Tia. Ask them to help me."

"Where are you, Rabbit? Where's Tia? What's wrong? Answer! Please, answer us!"

For a second Rabbit seemed to receive Ashira, then abruptly he broke off contact and the images faded.

18

In the morning Rabbit could walk, but it was obvious to Tia that the foot hurt a lot. To spare him extra exertion she gathered the mussels for their breakfast and broke them open for him. He was not very hungry and that worried her more than anything else. There was no water near the spot where they had spent the night, and Rabbit was unsatisfied with the remains of the fruit they had picked. When they finally set off it was more than an hour past dawn.

Rabbit limped along slowly, painfully. After a time the movement of the foot broke the clear scab which had formed during the night. The wound began to seep and sand collected on it. Rabbit gamely limped down to the edge of the sea and walked along in the water. Tia walked along close beside him, offering him her arm when he faltered. But he would not accept assistance.

"I'm nn-nn-not a baby," he told her, irritated, "I c-c-can go by m-myself. By t-t-tommorrow, it'll be all better and it won't hurt so much."

Cliffs hemmed the sea now. Starting as low banks of clay they had gradually grown into a high stone barricade between land and ocean, narrowing the beach to less than a few yards in some places. Slabs of rock broken and tumbled from the cliffs littered the sand and spilled out into the water where the waves crashed and poured over them.

Stopping early because Rabbit was exhausted, the children camped in a small inlet where a spring of fresh water sent a small waterfall running down the rock face. Two trees grew at the base of the cliff where the falls ended in a pool eroded out of the rock. The trees were twisted by the force of the sea winds and by the intermittent periods of drought when the spring in the rocks above dried up.

After drinking long and deeply, Rabbit abruptly fell asleep by the pool, his head almost in the water. Tia sat beside him for a time, worrying. He looked strange; his cheeks were very red, there were deep circles under his eyes and his neck seemed fatter than it should be. She felt his forehead; it was very warm and she loosened the drawstring at the neck of his shirt to make him cooler.

As she sat there it struck Tia she was hungry—and that she was tired of mussels. She looked up the side of the cliff. Great slabs of stone had fallen, creating ledges and slopes where the wind and rain had filled crevices with earth. She decided to climb the cliff and explore.

It was a fairly easy matter to get up to the top. Once there she paused to look back down. It was a long way to where Rabbit lay sleeping, straight down from where she stood. For a moment vertigo threatened and she stepped back from the edge of the cliff and threw herself flat against the ground. Reassured by the solidity of the earth, she felt the dizziness pass and in a few moments she sat up and surveyed the scene before her.

There had once been small dwellings here. There were still depressions and mounds in the slope, and the scattering of trees and plant growth left geometric areas barren except for coarse grasses. She walked over to the nearest tree, broke a dead branch from it and stuck the branch into the ground to mark her path back down to the cove. Then she began to explore.

Because she had the feeling they were going to be here for more than a night, she gathered anything she thought might be edible; small red berries from twisting aromatic vines, large yellow pulpy fruit from a number of trees, brownish wild oranges and insect-stung limes until the food sack was almost too heavy for her to lug.

By the time she returned to the cliff to start her descent, the only way she could manage to get the fruit down was to take out the sturdier pieces, drop them over the edge and hope they landed in the deep sand below.

Before attempting the descent she stood on the cliff edge and looked out. The ocean was bare of all but waves from horizon to horizon. Sighing, she slung the sack over her shoulder, tied the drawstrings around her neck, and began slipping and scrambling down the path. She would try very hard to reach Ashira before she went to sleep, she told herself.

Aside from the fact that Rabbit had turned over and lay on his back, he was in the same place she had left him. His mouth was open and he was breathing rapidly. She felt his forehead.

"He's burning up!"

Grabbing up the food sack she dumped out the fruit and ran down to the surf. Crabs scuttled away at her approach. She knelt at the water's edge, washed out the bag, rubbed it with wet sand and scraped it smooth with a broken shell, washed it out again and carried it, cold and dripping, to where the boy lay. When she had it wrapped around his foot, she collected smooth stones and placed them on both sides of Rabbit's leg and around the foot to keep it still and cool. Using an empty snail shell, she soaked the rocks and the wrapped leg repeatedly with cold water.

When that was finished she didn't know what else to do. She wished Ashira would come! It must be a lot more than a week since they left the Base—she tried to think back over the days but they ran together in her mind. Almost in despair her mind focused on one thought—Ashira.

Both Ashira and Varas answered so quickly she jumped.

"Where are you?" they asked immediately and simultaneously. "We have been trying to find you for days—why haven't you opened your mind?"

"I didn't know I had to," answered Tia, "I thought your pictures just came. . . ."

"Where are you?" they interrupted.

"I don't know—by The Sea—Rabbit is hurt. . . ."

"We know—he's been dreaming. But show us exactly where you are."

Tia showed them the cove, the rocks offshore, the beach in both directions.

"How many days have you been following the shore?"

She didn't know, couldn't remember.

"Let us see Rabbit—hold that image—keep showing us Rabbit, we'll try to get a fix. Good. Now the cove again—let us see the cove—from right to left again. . . ."

"Can't you help Rabbit?"

"Not until we reach you—but we'll be there soon. Have you seen anyone following you?"

"No—we lost them. When are you coming?"

"As fast as we possibly can. The coastline is full of coves and inlets that aren't on maps. We may lose valuable time locating the exact one you two are in. But keep in contact—we are less than a hundred miles south from you now. We must have passed you during the night."

"A hundred miles?" Tia wailed aloud as the fact sank into her troubled mind. A hundred miles might as well be a thousand—it had no meaning to her but vast distance. What little hope was left in her died like a candle guttering in a cold breeze. "Even if you ever find us now, Rabbit might. . . ." she could not associate the image of death with Rabbit.

"We will find you in time," Ashira promised over and over, not allowing herself to think of the men following the children's tracks. "You must believe that. Keep the boy cool and quiet. Under no circumstances is he to walk or even stand. We will be there soon—just stay with me now. Tia—Tia?"

But Tia shut them out. So far as she was concerned, she and Rabbit were alone. She still believed the ship might come. But in her life and experience, good things that "might be" had seldom, if ever, happened.

When full darkness came she lay down as close to Rabbit as she could get without disturbing him and put her skinny arms around him protectively. She slept little that night and each time she woke, she got up to pour cold water over the swollen foot. When Rabbit tried to twist away, the stones held him in place. By dawn he was very restless and only the sound of her voice seemed to comfort him.

When it was light enough to see she unwrapped the foot and looked at it. What she saw frightened her more. The foot had swollen until the toes stood splayed wide apart. There was a deep line across the foot at the base of the toes as though the skin wanted to stretch more and could not. The skin was an ugly reddish brown all around the wound and extending upward around the ankle.

When the sun was high enough to flood the little cove with heat, she dragged him over nearer the trees for shade. She squeezed two wild oranges until they were crushed inside, then tried to wake him and make him drink the juice.

"Rabbit, you must eat something. It'll make you feel better," she repeated over and over to him. But while he murmured in his unnatural sleep, she could not coax him to open his eyes. She opened the bruised fruit and pressed it against his lips, squeezing the pulp onto their cracked surface. He licked it off and she squeezed more until the orange was dry. She attempted to give him the second one but he twisted his face away.

She looked at him as he lay there, his face still, his breathing too shallow and quick, his body dry, hot, and a fear greater than any she had known before came over her. There was no doubt about it now—the ship would never come in time. Rabbit was going to die. She tried to reach his mind but nothing came to her. He had retreated deep within himself and all else was shut out.

Over her fear came a feeling of sadness quite beyond tears, and with the sadness, guilt. If she had not run away, Rabbit would still be safe. Or if she had refused to take him along he would have been punished, but he would be well and living and forgetting about her by this time. He had shared the Dreams—but she had made him believe they were real—when he would have probably dismissed it from his mind before the day was out. Why didn't she deny it? Why hadn't she left him locked in the root cellar? Why. . . ?

Lost in numbness she sat beside him until the sun was high in the sky and the tide reached its highest point. It was the spray from the waves that finally stirred her. She went to the spring and gathered a pad of wet moss to wash Rabbit's face and wet his lips.

19

She was sitting beside Rabbit when they appeared, walking in single file along the beach. For some minutes the men failed to see the two children they had hunted for so many miles. Perhaps it was only the sound of the water trickling down the cliff in a lull between waves that made one of the hunters stop and look towards the breach in the rocks.

"There they are!" he shouted.

Tia did not bother to rise as they angled across the beach and approached warily. And although she had believed them to have quit their pursuit, she was not really surprised to see them. Right now nothing much seemed to matter. She did note with satisfaction that the men still feared her and it faintly surprised her to know that their fear pleased her.

"Get away from the boy," the Major shouted when they were still some yards away.

"He's hurt—he's very sick. You must. . . ."

"Shut up! No one tells me what to do. Least of all you! Now get away from him."

Tia did not move. Rabbit moaned and tried to turn. The stone barricade restrained him.

"What's she done to him?" called Ed.

"How would I know, stupid?" snarled the Major. He took a hesitant step towards the two children. Tia watched him, her eyes narrow with hatred.

"Don't go no closer, sir," warned one of the men. "You don't know what she can do."

"I'm not afraid of a girl," said the Major. But he was afraid of this one and he stopped.

Counting on their fear to protect her, Tia rose stiffly to her feet. "If you promise to help him, I will. . . ."

She never got to finish the sentence. A rock thrown by one of the soldiers clunked against her temple. She felt a sharp pain, knew she was falling, and then nothing.

When she regained consciousness she was lying on her side against the cliff wall. Her hands and feet were securely tied behind her back, her dress pulled up over her mouth to gag her and tied. It was night, and the men had kindled a great fire of driftwood around which they all sat. She saw that Rabbit had been carried up close to the fire. "He'll be too hot!" she thought immediately and tried to move. But her bound arms prevented her from rolling onto her back, and the surge of pain that swept through her bruised head temporarily sickened her.

She found if she lay absolutely still her head did not hurt so much. After watching the fire for a time she closed her eyes. The men seemed to have forgotten about her, as though sure she could do them no harm in her present trussed condition. "I wonder what they are going to do to me," she thought. "Make me walk back to the Base? If they do—how will I walk with my ankles tied together?" But she didn't really care any more.

She had almost dozed off to sleep when she became aware that silence had fallen among the men. One of the soldiers stood up and walked down towards the water.

"There's green lights out there," he called—and Tia's heart went thomp!

"It's driftwood floating on the water," said the Major with self-assurance.

Two more men got up and went to look.

"They don't move like something just floating," reported one. "They move in a definite direction."

Tia saw the Major push himself to his feet and

join his men. The other three followed him. She tried to squirm into a sitting position but found she had been tied with such a short rope she could only lie jackknifed on her side.

"Whatcha think it is?"

"It's them!" Tia wanted to shout. "It's them! They *have* come for us!—for Rabbit and me!" But an innate sense of self-preservation kept her from betraying her knowledge. She looked over at her friend. He lay very still, the firelight flickering over his face leaving pools of shadow around his deep sunk eyes. "Please let him be alive," Tia prayed to the sky over her, "Please let him see we made it!" But the stars overhead blurred before her eyes and there was no answer.

One of the men moved uneasily away from the rest of the huddle. In the space left by him, Tia caught a glimpse of a tiny green light, far off shore. It winked twice and then disappeared behind a swell. She stared at the spot where it had been until her eyes hurt and she had to shut them to rest.

The men filed back towards the fire as though seeking reassurance from its warmth. "What do you think it is, sir?" Ed asked. As the leader of the group, the Major was responsible for providing a reassuring explanation of this unknown thing.

"Nothing," snapped the Major. "Some natural thing we don't know about. After all, what do we know of all this water? Maybe there are lightning bugs in the stuff like there are in the trees."

"I don't think so, begging your pardon, sir," Ed said. "They don't act like no bugs. They're on all the time and they seem to be getting closer all the time—and there's green ones and yellow ones in a straight line like they was lanterns set on a table."

"Maybe they come from another Base?"

The question came from the hunter, Oscar, who wore a leather band over his injured eye. "How do we know there weren't other Bases with people?"

The question hung in the air, frightening, unwanted, sacrilegious. The Major glared at Oscar, then, seeing he couldn't stare him down, shrugged.

"All right—if you men want to act like frightened females, pick up your arms! Hide yourself behind the rocks until the nasty lights go away again and the sun comes out. This water is nothing more than a source of salt. If you hunters were a little braver you could have found it years ago instead of walking miles into the hills. Now you need some new excuse to keep away from it, don't you?"

"I ain't scared of the water," lied Oscar, "but I think it would be smart to put out this fire. No sense asking for trouble until we know what them lights are." He began to kick sand onto the flames.

"No!" shouted the Major. Suddenly furious, he stepped threateningly towards the man, his arm raised to strike if Oscar spoke again. "No! You will all do what I say. I am the Major! You are standing here miles from the Base, scared by something you know nothing about. And because you are frightened, you act like Simples! Now just sit down and control yourselves!" He paused, noting the men seemed to doubt him. "You heard what I said—SIT DOWN AND ACT LIKE MEN!" he roared in fury.

Trained to respect the ultimate authority of a Major, the men slowly sat, not willingly, but obediently. After a moment the Major joined them on the sand.

Tia watched him sitting there, like a bearded brown toad staring at the fire, seemingly ignoring his men and their sullen faces. He threw a clam into the flames and she could hear it crack and sizzle. He raked it out, opened it and shoved the meat into his mouth. The raw rubbery flesh displeased him and he spat it back into the flames. She shut her eyes as she saw him turn to look back towards where she lay.

"I think I know where our lights come from!" he announced, his voice artificially loaded with insinuating threat. "I know why we think we see them."

"But she's still out cold," objected Oscar. "What could she do?"

"You're pretty dumb, aren't you? You thought she was almost drowned when she put out your eye, too." Ed's tone was mocking.

"Someone go get her," commanded the Major.

No man moved from his seat.

"I said, go get her!" The Major was getting angry again. "All right, if you're afraid—I'll get her myself." He rose awkwardly and Tia heard him coming towards her over the sand. She pretended to be asleep.

He grabbed her arm and jerked her up onto her knees. The thongs cut into her wrists and ankles, and she involuntarily cried out in pain.

"So you are awake!" He shook her roughly. "And this is your doing!" He spoke loudly for the men's benefit more than hers. "Answer me! You put those lights out there, didn't you?"

Tia said nothing. He slapped her and only the gag kept her from biting her tongue. Then, abruptly, he let her slip through his grasp to the ground and awkwardly knelt down on one knee in front of her, his back to the fire and the men.

As he leaned over to pull down her gag she

smelled the sourness of his body under the leather gown. His face was in shadow; she could see only tiny points of light in his eyes as they searched her face. She had never been so near to him before, nor so frightened of him.

When he spoke again, his soft cajoling whisper came as a shock. "You can save yourself a lot of grief, girl. Tell me how you killed Otto. Tell me what power you used." When she did not answer, he said, "If you tell me, I promise not to hurt you. I won't even punish you for half-blinding one of my best men. You can come back to the Base . . . nothing more will happen to you."

"Nothing will happen to me because I'll be dead," thought Tia. She kept silent.

"You're frightened, that's why you won't talk. But trust me. The others think you're a witch— they want me to kill you. But we know better, don't we? You're smart like me. You and I know things . . . when I was your age I used to be able to tell. . . ." He paused as though considering just how much of himself he should betray in confidence to gain what he wanted to know.

"Major—the lights quit moving!" The call came from down the beach.

"She decided to be good, Major?" asked Ed. "That why the lights stopped?"

"They're lots closer now." That was Oscar's voice.

As though hoisted by panic, the Major scrambled erect and whirled about to look out over the sea. By straining her neck to see around his legs, Tia caught a glimpse of green and yellow shining on the waves.

"If you've done this, I'll kill you right here," the Major promised her. He stood above her, stinking of fearsweat and breathing heavily, his hands clenched at his sides.

Tia lay sick with fear, so absorbed by it that she thought she was dreaming when Varas' thought reached her.

"Don't cry out, Tia.— Are you there by the fire?"

She didn't answer the first time and he repeated both the warning and the question. With effort she thought "yes" and knew his relief.

"Good! We have found you in time! Is the boy alive?"

He received her emotion-charged images of Rabbit. For a moment he wavered and became unclear and she was afraid she had lost him. Then he responded again.

"We must train you to control your power—especially at close range. You think the boy is alive but you are not sure—is that correct?"

"Yes!" Tia tried to raise her head and look out to sea.

"Lie still. Keep your eyes closed. We do not want you to attract any more of their attention." His mind left hers abruptly.

"There's something moving out there on the water!" came a shout. The Major ran heavily towards the sea for a better look.

"Where?"

"There—beyond the rocks—just there—see it?"

"It's big!"

"It's got white lights!"

"Put out that fire!"

"It's the witch!" shouted the Major. "She's doing it. It's not something real—it can't be!"

"We'll soon see if it is." Ed grabbed a thick branch of firewood and started towards Tia.

20

"STOP!—*I will not re-
peat the warning!*"

Amplified, it was the voice of a giant that echoed
off the water and reverberated from the cliffs. In
the silence that followed, the waves went on crashing against the rocks offshore.

Ed, who had paused in fright, now regained his
confidence and took three running steps forward.
There was a zinging sound and he fell and lay
still. Shouts of dismay and anger came from the
men only to be interrupted by the voice.

*"Any man who attempts to harm either child
will die!"*

"But it's only a woman's voice," one of the men
realized, puzzled.

"Kill the witch!" the Major hissed.

Oscar was so desperately frightened of the voice

he jumped to obey. There was another "zing" and he, too, dropped onto the sand. After that the five left stood afraid to move, waiting for whatever the witchcraft would bring next.

Minutes passed and nothing happened. Stiff with tension, Tia waited and strained her eyes looking into the watery darkness beyond the camp-fire. The Major suddenly dropped to the ground and began to crawl towards the fire. Tia saw him begin pushing sand onto the flames. She wanted to tell Varas what the Major was doing but she was afraid she would hurt the man as she had done last time when she was telling him about Rabbit, so she blanked out her thoughts by focusing on a stone lying near her face. The fire grew smaller and dimmer and then, with one broad kick of his leg, the Major smothered it with sand until only a few branches and coals glowed red in the breeze.

In the darkness she saw him stand. Clutched in his right hand was a heavy driftwood branch, the end of it still glowing from the fire. He half turned, as though measuring the distance separating them, and then with a kind of desperation, he ran towards her. She saw him loom over her and as he swung, she rolled sideways. The glowing club made a fiery arc. It hit the rock wall behind her with savage force that sent a shower of burning sparks cascading to the sand. He "oofed" with the impact but whirled around, seeking to understand how he could have missed. Tia desperately flopped herself backwards in the sand away from him, made an awkward lunge for his legs as the club swung up. The weight of her body threw him off stride and he missed again.

There was a brilliant flash of light; the entire cove seemed momentarily illuminated as though by lightning, but the source was not the clouds. Tia glanced up and saw the expression on the Major's face fade from rage to terror. In an instant he turned and fled up over the rocks to the cliff, climbing as fast as his fat would allow him. As he disappeared over the top, Tia turned her head and with a shock, saw what had frightened him.

A huge beetle-like thing rolling on six wide wheels was approaching the ruins of the fire. It had a gleaming white carapace like two folded wings surmounted by a crystal clear top, clear chiton seemed to cover the eye-like bulbous lights on the front and rear.

Its sudden appearance would have been enough to panic the already frightened men, but its resemblance to an enormous insect totally terrified them. Shielding their eyes from the blinding headlights, the four of them ran shrieking, jumping over their two fallen companions lying in the sand, mad to escape.

A searchlight made a swift circle of the campsite, pausing for a moment at each figure lying on the ground, then flashed up the cliff face and swept along it. As the thing rolled to a stop, the top winged open and two people dressed in strange garments jumped down onto the sand. Almost before the door closed, the vehicle moved off after the four men who were running north along the beach. The cove was left in darkness once more.

Temporarily blinded by the change from daylight back to night, Tia lay in the dark and listened for the approach of footsteps. She wanted to call out—but she was suddenly caught up with shyness. What must she look like to people like this? In the distance she heard one of the fleeing men scream like a rabbit caught in a snare and she shivered.

A torch on the belt of one of the strangers threw a circle of light on Rabbit's body. No sooner had the light flashed on than a rock hit the beach near where they stood. Instantly two beams of light swept across the cove and up. The strangers jumped to one side as another rock thudded into the sand next to Rabbit's head. Tia saw one of them reach for something hanging at his belt. There was a shiny glint and a zinging sound.

A heavy wave crashed against the rocks offshore and poured its volume up onto the sand. As it receded she heard a scrambling noise above her and involutarily jumped as the Major's body came hurtling down to land with a sharp cracking sound on the stones by the pool of the little spring.

As the two white-clad figures ran to the body, the girl received images of bones jaggedly broken, of blood welling out of ruined tissue, the thoughts of a dying mind filled with fear and hatred for herself, for Rabbit, and regret that he had not killed them both. She saw the two of them as infants, saw the faces of her mother and a woman she had never known. And by some cold intuition she knew that because she could receive these images, the Major had been like herself and Rabbit.

The knowledge, his hatred, his death, soured through her body and she retched and was sick on the sand.

Dimly through the tears of nausea she saw a torch flash towards her. With great effort she pushed sand over the vomitus with her elbow, then attempted to sit up as the stranger hurried over and dropped to both knees before her. The light raked over her twisted body. She closed her eyes against the glare and turned her face away, partially in shyness, partially in shame lest this person had seen or heard her throw up. A hand gently touched her face and turned it. The light was put down on the sand.

"Tia?" The voice was low, the accent very strange. "Tia?"

"Yes?"

"I am Ashira."

Tia opened her eyes and stared up at the woman's face. It was half-hidden by the soft hood that fell forward around it, but the girl recognized it as the face she had seen in her Dreams for so many long years, the face she always suspected she had only imagined with its elegant nose and eyes so dark they looked black in this light—eyes regarding her now with compassion and something more she could not understand but only feel.

"I am Ashira." The phrase came again unspoken and with it the promise, "You are safe now in our being."

What she had wished for so long had come and she felt the fear go out of her in an immense sigh of relief, and the sigh ended in a sob. And Tia, who never cried no matter how hard she was hit or how badly she was hurt or humiliated or teased, cried now.

She was only vaguely aware when Ashira cut the thongs, releasing her hands and then her legs, and aware only because she could cover her face with her numb hands to try and stifle the sobs escaping from her throat. She cried as though it was an act of shame, a weakness she hated but could no longer control. When Ashira tried to take her in her arms, she twisted away from the woman and buried her face in the sand to hide the weakness.

Ashira had had ample occasion during this voyage to become familiar with the feeling of helplessness. But she had never felt so inadequate as now. To compensate for her inability to aid in any better way, she began rubbing the circulation back into Tia's legs.

"What is wrong? Is she badly hurt?"

"No, not seriously, Varas. She's in shock. She needs the relief of weeping. How is Rabbit?"

"Alive," he said, and then to spare Tia, he switched to their private thoughts. "He has a massive infection and he is severely dehydrated. That right foot is huge— I can't really see in this light. We must find one of those snails and analyze it as soon as we get back to the ship. Did you see those . . . men? Did you get a good look at them?"

"Yes, and I received the last thoughts of the one

I shot." Ashira shivered. "Somehow I never thought we'd use target pistols on living things."

Varas nodded grimly. Like Ashira, he found violence repulsive. "At least we know who sired both children. Are we going on to their Base?"

"No. I want Tia and Rabbit safely back at Morrow as soon as possible. After seeing the men here tonight, I'm in no hurry to see the rest. The Major knew what these two children were. He feared no others."

"So you think he sired no others with the Morrow gene?"

"Don't you?"

"Yes," Varas admitted, "but I would like to see those people to make sure."

"You shall. You can lead another expedition here as soon as we can spare you—one properly equipped to stay and study, if you wish."

"Here comes Mark."

Tia's thin eyelids registered a beam of light flashing across the cove as the amphibian returned.

"Shall we take Tia to the car first?" she heard Varas ask.

"I think so. Tia—don't bother to answer—we're going to take you and Rabbit back to the ship now. Can you walk?"

Tia felt a hand on her shoulder and she rolled over and sat up. Varas handed her a soft cloth and gently flashed the suggestion that she use it to wipe her eyes and nose.

"I'm O.K. . . . I'm . . . sorry to be. . . ." she was still jerking from the sobs as she blew her nose.

"Shhhh—there is nothing to apologize for. Come with us." Ashira was restraining her urge to comfort for fear of releasing another emotional storm in Tia. The child was too near physical collapse to cope with feeling.

She was led, half supported by the two adults, to the door of the sea-land car. Then, remembering, she broke away from the pair and stumbled across the sand to where three people bent over Rabbit's still form. They had cut off his clothes and he lay naked in the wind. She knelt in the sand beside him. Almost immediately Varas and Ashira were at her side again.

"Will he get well?" Tia whispered. He looked so pale in this bright light, hair black against his skin, lips swollen and cracked, skinny ribs sticking up from his chest. The person who sat leaning over him, apparently listening to his insides with some sort of metallic tube hanging from the ears, glanced over at the girl. Everyone was dressed alike in their trousered garments with hoods; Tia could not tell if this was a man or a woman until it spoke.

"I don't know if he will live," the woman said bluntly, "but from the looks of you, I'd say you can both live through quite a lot. Now go get into the car. I'll bring your brother in a moment."

"He's not my brother—he's my friend." The distinction was very important to her. In her experience brothers were never friends.

The woman glanced at her again quizzically, then smiled and nodded as if it didn't really matter. "You go get in the car," she repeated. "We'll take good care of him."

"We will follow you, Lora," Ashira said quietly and put her arm around the girl.

Tia watched as two people deftly slid a blanket beneath Rabbit, lifted him gently and laid him onto a stretcher, being careful not to move his injured foot. A yellow cover was put over him and secured to the sides of the stretcher and he was carried to the car, Lora at his side, the rest following. The crystal cover on the car swung open at the rear; the stretcher was slid inside on two grooves built to hold it.

"Can you see if you leave my dome lights on?"

the doctor called to someone in the front of the vehicle. "I want to start an IV."

"Right," came the call. "We have a snail for you, too."

"Come, Tia." Varas took her hand, "we'll ride up here. Rabbit is in good care now."

She was led around to the side of the car and lifted into it to sit on one of the benchlike seats built into its walls. Ashira and Varas sat on either side of her.

"Are we going to leave the beach like this?" she heard a man call as a searchlight panned over the area and lit on the three bodies still lying there. "There's four more down further."

"Good," commented Ashira, "We don't want to return to find an army. We'll clean up the beach in the morning. Let's go."

The rest of the party climbed inside, the doors were sealed. The car made a smooth turn and headed south down the narrow beach to a point where the rocks permitted entry into the sea. As they wallowed into the swells, Tia noticed a definite rocking motion that reminded her of the wild ride on the tree and she stiffened in fear.

"It's all right," Ashira reassured her. "You're safe." She wrapped a blanket around the girl.

Tia relaxed a bit. Water hit the windshield as they sped through the waves, a bar came up and brushed it away again and again. The girl watched it in fascination. It was hard to see out with the lights on inside. She looked back to see if she could tell how Rabbit was but the three people were clustered around him blocking her view.

There were lights visible outside now. The speed of the amphibian slowed almost to a stop and it began to wallow again. There was a clunking sound as the car struck against something gently, then they seemed to be going up. She heard a highpitched whine and then another, louder clunk and they had stopped. They were on the ship.

She yawned involuntarily as the door opened again and Varas jumped out and helped her to the deck. There was a small crowd waiting for them. Strange hands reached out to offer their aid.

"We have them both," she heard Ashira say and then she didn't remember that they said anything else. Perhaps she fell asleep then or, more likely, she thought later, they stopped using verbal speech in favor of mental communication. She remembered being led down a narrow corridor to a tiny room and given a glass of some cool liquid before she fell into a deep sleep.

2 1

It was six long days before she was allowed to see Rabbit. And when she had time to think, she worried each one of those days. The medical staff told her, of course, that he was getting better, but until she was allowed to talk to him herself, she didn't quite believe them.

Ashira had temporarily put her into the care of the doctors and, while Tia had to admit they were kind to her, their ministrations both embarrassed and at times frightened her.

She was fed and mended. She was soaked and scrubbed and trimmed and clipped. She was examined by three different people and a person called a biogeneticist who was also a doctor of some sort—but Tia was not yet sure what. All she knew was that the woman was very fond of taking samples of her. Just when the girl thought she was through with doctors, another appeared to work on her teeth.

When she was finally allowed to dress, Tia was given hooded daysuits like everyone else wore, and to her amusement, underwear. And when she was told that all the clothing she wore was to be put in the laundry daily, she suddenly understood why they all looked so clean.

Because her hair had to be cut quite short to get rid of all the burrs and snarls, it lay now in layers of gentle curls around her face. The first time she put on a lime-green daysuit and looked at herself in a full length mirror, it took her a long moment to realize she was seeing her own reflection. And then she was very pleased! If only Rabbit could see her.

There was so much to learn and see, everything from faces and names to food and flush toilets and how to make her own bed. Ashira wanted her to be shown only the necessities as yet, feeling this should be a recuperative period, but even the basics were almost too much to comprehend at once. And with everything new she was shown or given, Tia wished she could share it with Rabbit.

"But why can't I see him?" she asked Ashira and Varas for the four hundredth time.

"Because he is in a sterile room. . . ." They

tried to explain it to her but there was still too much of a gap in her knowledge.

"But is he getting well? He doesn't answer my thoughts."

"He's been too ill—give him a little time and he will recover."

But after a few days her initial enthusiasm about her new life, her new friends, and even the marvel of the big ship itself wore thin with worry.

Finally on the afternoon of the sixth day, the mass of tubes that had saved and supported Rabbit's life were removed, and Lora came personally to find Tia and tell her the good news.

"He's still a little dopey," she warned the happy girl, "but you can talk to him for a few minutes."

When Tia entered he was half sitting up in a narrow bed, his injured foot covered by a small tent. For a long moment the two children stared at one another, half shy, half dumbstruck at seeing how different they looked.

"Rabbit—are you O.K.?" Tia finally managed to ask, although she could see that he was.

"B-b-boy!" he exploded, "do-do you ever look p-p-pretty! Oh Tia—I b-bet you're as p-pretty as anybody here!" He cocked his head to get a better look at her. "They c-cut your hair, too. Did you see mine?"

"You look pretty, too, Rabbit. They. . . ."

"And my ff-fingernails—did you see my f-finger-nails?" He held out his hands for inspection. "I d-didn't know they were that white color at the ends all the t-time—did you?"

Tia nodded yes, and checked her own hands just to make sure they looked as nice.

Suddenly quiet, as though remembering something, Rabbit reached out for Tia's hand and held it tightly. "I'm s-so glad to ss-see you!" he said and his chin quivered in spite of his obvious efforts to control it. "When I woke up I was ss-so scared! They had all these t-tubes in me—even in my nn-nose—and I d-d-didn't know what had happened to me or where you were—or where I wa-was. I thought I was d-d-d-d-dead, maybe." He swallowed hard.

"These p-people kept c-calling to m-me. I w-wanted to s-sleep—but they k-kept calling me. They knew my n-name so I figured you—you had to be around to tell them that—b-but you d-d-didn't come and you didn't come s-so I thought m-maybe you d-d-died . . ." Big tears escaped and made wet tracks down his round little face.

With tears in her own eyes Tia impulsively plumped down on his bed and hugged him close to her. "I've been trying to see you ever since we got on board, Rabbit."

"On board what? Wh-where are we? We're m-moving—where are w-we going?"

"We're on the ship," she began rather lamely, "we're going to. . . ." She paused—where were they going really?

The door to the room slid open to admit Ashira and Varas. At the sight of the children together they smiled.

"Hi," Rabbit greeted them, "I nn-know you— you were in mm-my dream! Do you know wh-where we're going?"

"We're going home, Rabbit," said Ashira. "We're all going home."

ORDINARY JACK
Helen Cresswell

The first book in the Bagthorpe Saga, about the entertaining, eccentric and exasperating Bagthorpe family. Jack is the only ordinary member of the talented family and even his dog is branded as thick – then Uncle Parker thinks of a scheme to win him all the attention he craves, but it doesn't always work out as smoothly as planned.

ELEANOR, ELIZABETH
Libby Gleeson

Eleanor has been wary of her new home so far: the landscape is strange and the faces in the classroom unfriendly. Then, her new life changes completely with the discovery of her grandmother's old diary. Now, with a bush fire rampaging just behind them, her life and the lives of Ken, Mike and six-year-old Billy depend on how she uses what she *has* learned about this alien world. She needs help, and only her grandmother, sixty-five years away, can give it to her.